T0104434

Melange

WILLIAM ADEE

authorHOUSE®

AuthorHouse™ UK Ltd.
1663 Liberty Drive
Bloomington, IN 47403 USA
www.authorhouse.co.uk
Phone: 0800.197.4150

Published by AuthorHouse   04/24/2014

ISBN: 978-1-4969-7822-6 (sc)
ISBN: 978-1-4969-7823-3 (e)

This book is dedicated to my late daughter Deborah

Contents

Diamond Jim 1

Espansa 20

Friends 42

Grandma 68

Invalids United 78

Little Animals 104

My Cursed Day 109

My Day 114

My Gentle Love 130

Our Utopia 135

Rebels 177

Revenge 209

Tales Of Fairyland 215

That's Life 220

The Mine 232

Stuff Them 241

DIAMOND JIM

*W*e thought that we, that's my mate, Rob, Rob is six feet tall, broad shouldered, and Blonde, and me, I'm Chris by the way, I'm six feet tall, slim, brown haired.

Anyway, we thought that we would go on a holiday of a lifetime, after having saved hard for a whole year or more, as we would never be able to do it again, because Rob was getting married next year. We had been mates from school days even worked together; we knew each other pretty well. This was our last chance to do something we had wanted to do for a long time, we would be taking two months off work, and this was a special arrangement with our firm, I'm glad to say. Or it would not have been possible, and as we were going to be hiking around the world, or as far as we could when our two months were up, but with a little help, like flying to a country, exploring what we wanted to see, then on to the next country and so on. First we flew to Nigeria, and intended to hike to Ghana, just to see some of Africa, down south was far too dangerous, and from there we were going to Egypt, we landed in Lagos, went through customs, and out into the sweltering heat. With a journey of about three hundred miles trek, were we mad or what, as we walked out of the airport, and looked around, we were approached by an African he was slim six feet tall dark curly haired, "need a guide" he said, in pigeon English smiling, "very good guide and cheap" "okay, how much" we agreed a price and decided to call him Ned, as his name was unpronounceable to us. We showed him on our map where we wanted to go, "Okay, jeep be ready in one hour" and left, "jeep" Rob said in surprise, "I thought we were walking".

"yeah" I answered back, "but walk in this heat, you cannot be serious old mate, besides, we can see a lot more with a jeep, and visit places we wouldn't have been able to before" "I suppose so" Rob replied, a bit sad.

We left the airport steps and went to have a coffee at a nearby café, or whatever there called here, we sat down out side and waited for Ned to return.

I knew that Rob was disappointed he had wanted to walk, and had been looking forward to it, but he would soon cheer up, when we were on our way.

Ned turned up in about an hour as he said, and joined us at our table, we talked for a while of different places to visit, some off the beaten track, that he knew, and his fee was cheap.

I wondered about that, but kept quiet, I would be keeping an eye on him anyway, we loaded the jeep, checked with the local police to register our journey, and then we were off.

We had been traveling for about two hours, when I asked Ned to "stop for a cup of tea" which he did, while it was brewing, I just lay down on the ground, watching the smoke drifting lazily upwards, Rob was sitting up in the shade of a tree, when we heard another engine, "someone coming" Rob shouted, as I looked up, it stopped, out got an army officer and two soldiers.

They spoke to Ned in African, and then he spoke to us, "Passports and visas please gentlemen" the officer said, these we gave him, along with the police visa we had been given.

Okay, have a nice journey, but watch out for any rebels" Saluting he left and they drove off.

I looked at Ned; he seemed a bit nervous, "hmm" I thought "I wonder why" we finished our tea and continued our journey, off the beaten track this time. I was a bit concerned, "we go to a village" Ned shouted over the roar of the engine,

Rob was happily videoing the scenery, as we bumped along for a couple more hours, coming to a hilltop, we could see a village below, mud huts and all, but a wooden building stood at the side.

"Ha" I thought "civilization at last" we had only been traveling one day, chiefs home" said Ned, as we pulled up beside it, "good place to stay tonight".

"Can we film around the village" Rob asked, just as a man appeared in the door way, six feet tall and chubby, he nodded and said "jambo" Ned answered, "yes we could" so off Rob went, to do his stuff.

I think he videoed everything in sight, even goats eating, he was well pleased at the end of the day, I had looked around, but kept an eye on Ned, he was talking to the chief who handed him a wad of money, which he slipped into his coat pocket, I ducked back behind a hut and walked out around the other side, when they saw me the chief said "food soon" "right" I replied, all innocent.

And went to fetch Rob, then we all sat down to eat, it tasted like chicken, but in rather large pieces, so I doubt it was, probably ostrich, but Rob nor I wanted to know what it really was, we were hungry, we talked to the chief for a few hours, with Ned as translator, and found that he had two sons at a private school in England.

How can he afford it, I thought, there's nothing here, unless smuggling something, so that's why Ned was nervous of the soldiers, hope it's not drugs I'd hate that, so would Rob.

We went to bed eventually, completely washed out with the heat, were not acclimatized yet, Rob snored his head off all night, I slept fitfully and was still tired in the morning, "come on lazy bones" Rob shouted, "get up breakfasts ready" I hate people who are cheerful first thing, it takes me half an hour and two cuppers to be awake, "piss off" I replied, he tipped me out of bed, "come on get a shower" "a shower out here" I thought, but a bucket with holes in it, is just as good, except the waters cold, I had a shower anyway, then to the loo, if you can call it one, and to breakfast, the same chicken as last night, "oh well its food anyway" this done, we loaded up the jeep said our farewells and were off, "a good idea this jeep" Rob remarked, as we bumped along, I just nodded and pointed to some monkeys playing in a tree, Rob got his video going, "good".

He pointed, "Nice shot of them" we traveled till midday, and then stopped for a cupper beside a river, "can we swim in there" "yes" Ned replied "no crocodiles" "come on Rob beat you in". But I only just made it, as we swam around in our nakedness, "teas up" Ned shouted, "me first" I said, well, until Rob pushed me back in, "get you next time" I yelled, while they both stood there laughing.

After a rest we bumped along again, dirty, dusty, soaked with sweat and flies, cooling off just didn't last long, I thought and wondered about our guide Ned, what was he up to, I had to find out but carefully, very carefully.

We were now nearing a place called "Koforidua," Ned informed us, beside Lake Volta" which is about two thirds of the way to Accra.

Here we spent a few days; we went exploring and recording the scenery, especially a view from the dam, stunning sight.

when we said that we wanted to move on, Ned announced "that he was going to Abidjan, then to his own village a few miles further on, and that we were welcome to come for the ride, and that he would take us to Accra airport from there, and that there were some beautiful sights to see".

Rob was all for it, but I hesitated, "come on" Rob chided, "lets do it" "Okay" so next morning we set off for Abidjan, but still on outback roads, another two hundred and fifty miles of dust, bumps and flies.

We must have been mad to do it, but we did, Rob was on his fifth camcorder film, only two more left he said, he was really enjoying it, I was but to a point, there was still a nagging doubt in my mind, but I kept an eye on Ned.

We stopped that night at another mud hut village, Rob did some filming, while I looked around, hmm, I thought not much in the way of fields, but plenty of food around though, what's the catch to all this.

Now my curiosity really got the better of me, I really had to find out, the next morning we continued on our journey, the scenery was good and pleasant to see.

That evening we stopped at a town called Dunkwa, and rented rooms, nice beds and drinks were in order, at the time we were enjoying our drinks, in came an army officer.

The same one we had met a few days ago, I invited him over for a drink, Ned was really nervous this time, and left saying "that he had to get the jeep filled and ready for the morning" "funny" I thought, "he only filled it up this afternoon, from the jerry cans that were carried on the jeep".

me and rob chatted to the officer we informed him "that we were going to Abidjan, then returning to Accra to continue our trip" "lucky you" he said, "being able to afford it" then we explained, "Oh well once in a lifetime, I might do that myself, That's a good idea you have, but I'll miss out Africa I think" at this we all laughed, we had a pleasant evening together, then said our goodbyes to Tristan the army officer.

Went to our room and crashed out, completely shattered, we were woken by Ned at six o'clock, "come on time to get going" he shook Rob, who nearly fell out of bed, "bloody hell, wake a bloke up gently" he grumbled, "we must go before it gets too hot" Ned muttered, "I wait outside for half hour, no more Okay" we got up splashed our faces with water dressed and went to meet Ned, "what's his hurry today" I asked, "dunno, but it had better be good" Rob muttered, we collected our gear and went to the jeep.

Ned seemed agitated and annoyed, "took your time" he grumbled as we climbed in, and off we went at top speed.

"got out of bed the wrong side" I said, sitting up in the back after being thrown over by a bump in the road, "sorry" he said, "got to meet someone, and I'm late, hang on" we bounced along at break neck speed for an hour, then we met up with an old fellow, who was sitting by a large tree, we pulled up sharply, Ned jumped out.

"Glad we made it" he uttered, giving the old man a hug, turning to us "it's my father, he's going away today, and I just had to see him" "Ok" we chimed, "it's understandable, if you'd only said before".

they talked for a while then the old man got up and walked away, Ned just stood there looking after him, till he was out of sight, then he turned with tears in his eyes. "I'll make tea and breakfast now" and set about the task in hand, he said "sorry" again over breakfast, but Rob just passed it off.

"When can I film some more" he asked, "as soon as were on our way" Ned replied, "we'll be at my village in half an hour".

when we arrived there were shouts of joy, "jambo" "jambo" they were all laying, I found out later that Ned was their chief, who brought money to feed the village people to survive, and going away was going to die, we were honored guests that night, talk about killing the fatted calf, what a feast, and drink, I don't remember going to bed that night, nor does Rob, but the next morning, what a head, the worst hangover I've ever had, must be the local brew, a type of gin I think it took all day for our heads to clear.

by evening feeling better, we were hungry and ate quite a lot, genuine chicken this time, and we only drank tea, the following morning Ned announced "that we should be going back the following day" morning came we "have to make one more stop" said Ned, hmm, I wondered, the day passed pleasant enough, with Ned getting the jeep ready with provisions, fuel and water for the return journey.

"Come on we must go" said Ned, late afternoon, funny time to go I mused, as we left we waved goodbye to the villagers, but not many around though, we left the village stopped for a cupper, Ned was checking the jeep.

"We have to stay here tonight, leaky" and went out into the bush, again avoiding the main road, about seven o'clock, "the radiator I will fix it when it cools down" he gestured; suspicious I said to myself didn't see any steam.

Ned tinkered with the jeep into the late evening Rob and me we just wandered around and rested in the shade, having finished the jeep, Ned said "early start in the morning Okay".

But he looked a bit worried to me, Rob said "Okay," I just nodded in agreement, but wondered why, and should I voice my suspicions to Rob.

As we wandered around, and Rob was filming the sunset scene from a hill top, I told him of my suspicions, "I knew something was going on, but wasn't sure what" he said, "and I didn't want to alarm you either".

"So well both keep an eye on him from now on" "Okay" as we walked back to camp for supper, we arranged to sleep in shifts from now on.

After supper Rob went to sleep, as my shift was first, then wake him at about two o'clock, this way we both would get some sleep, about midnight I settled down in my sleeping bag, pretending to sleep, eyes closed but ears open. In fact I did doze off, but woke up on hearing a movement around us, opening one eye, I could just see Ned picking up a small sack from the jeep, then looking around to check on us, I closed my eyes quick, and then he walked away from the camp.

I cautiously got up after a few minutes, tucked up my sleeping bag to look like I was still in it, got out the binoculars and watched Ned, "wake up" I whispered to Rob, nudging him with my foot.

time for my watch" he said sleepily, "no I've been watching Ned, and he's just gone for a walkabout with some small sacks, I'm going to follow him, how about you".

Luckily it was just light enough to see, without falling over your feet, as we followed him at a distance and keeping watch through the binoculars.

He came to the top of a small rise, laid down on his belly in the bushes.

We stopped and knelt down behind more bushes, although there wasn't much cover really, "has he seen us" I muttered to Rob, "no were too far away mate besides, we've got the gun haven't we".

"he's crawling forwards now, over the hilltop" Rob said giving me a running commentary, "come on" so quietly as we could we crept to the place on the rise where Ned had been.

Lying on our bellies we peered over the top, a barbed wire fence met our gaze, with a danger sign on it, minefield it read, we waited until we saw Ned appear from under the barbed wire, slithering up the slope and over the top and straight into us.

As I pointed the gun at him the look on his face was one of disbelief, and amazement, he said something in African, probably swearing at us, then in his broken English, "let's get down the slope then I'll explain".

We went down the slope and sat down, Ned was very nervous, not knowing what we would do with him.

"Okay, past the mine field is a small beach, half a mile long, it's part of a diamond mine, small diamonds are littered every where, some on the surface even, I collect them once a year and use them to keep the villages alive, especially the ones that you've seen".

"yeah" I said interrupting, "we wondered why they were all so healthy looking, and no crops around" Ned then carried on talking, "I collect money from the big chief," like the first one I had seen giving Ned money.

"The chief had two sons at a private school in England, the money helps the villagers survive, and the diamonds help pay for it all, also it keeps the boys at school in England.

To give them a better chance in life than just living in mud huts, my boy is included also, there you have it, it's a bit of smuggling that helps a lot of people and it doesn't hurt anyone".

"So now you can have me arrested, or just go home and forget what you have seen" "hmm" I mumbled, putting the safety catch on the gun, and lowering it to the ground, "as I see it" I voiced my thoughts, "unless we help you and maybe ourselves, a lot of people will suffer, right" "right" Rob replied.

"But risky if you are caught by the guards, it will mean a long jail sentence" Ned cautioned, "we came for adventure, and the risky bit well that'll just make it all the more better for us won't it" I conjectured.

But I added, "only on the condition that I come with you to pick our own stones" "you can't" said Rob, "and I'm not risking my neck or yours" said Ned, so we argued for a while, "Okay, Okay, if you want to risk your life, that's fine by me, but if anything happens, I'm gone".

"fair enough" I agreed, "Rob can keep a look out, he's getting married next year, so he's definitely not coming with us, are you" I almost shouted at him, "keep your voices down or we'll be caught before we get started" he warned as Rob knew I could be a stubborn old bugger once my mind was made up.

so he didn't argue, "if anything happens you take this bag of diamonds to my village" he pointed in a direction, "that way about four hours drive, don't worry, you'll be safe, they'll know what to do" "yeah" I added, "go like a bat out of hell" Rob nodded, with his usual look of disapproval.

At me doing something that I shouldn't be doing.

He's got me out of a few tight spots in the past, and I didn't expect him to run away this time either, whatever happens, "cos he's a stubborn old sod like me".

This I was thinking as I got ready to follow Ned into the unknown, as we slithered down the slope snake like, as we went Ned was giving me instructions we got to the barbed wire, Ned was talking in a whisper, "sound carries a long way at night" he muttered, "so keep your head down.

And follow me, whichever way I go, do something different and you'll be blown to bits" we slid under the wire and into the mine field, as I followed Ned on my belly, weaving through the mines, I was sweating and scared, and I needed a wee, as Ned said "stay calm and you'll be alright" I could just see him in front of me.

When we reached the beach Ned called me to him, "no mines here, but don't pick any bigger than this size" he showed me one, "titchy little thing" I thought, "it's plenty big enough milky white stone uncut diamond".

Not what I expected, "now fill your bag and meet me back here in a few minutes" as I looked around I could see little gleams of light in the sand.

I filled my bag and met up with Ned again, "come on" he whispered, "back we go follow me and don't forget what I said" "as if I would" I thought, and needed a wee more than ever now, once we got back to where Rob was waiting, I went behind a bush, what a relief, I never wanted a wee so much before.

"My turn now" Rob whispered, I'm not missing all the excitement, what do you think I am" I bloody well knew it" I thought "stubborn old bugger" I just chuckled, "I know" I said, as off they went.

While I kept watch, I was more nervous than them in the minefield, at last they came back up the slope, after what seemed like hours, "come on" Ned said, "back to camp sun up soon it's best to be away from here before the army patrols come".

I noticed that Rob had gone behind a bush, "I know what your doing" I mused to myself, we got back to the jeep, threw everything on board, Ned was covering the bonnet with blankets to quieten down the sound of the engine. Off we went not as fast as usual, but a pace for about an hour, then we stopped, Ned got out "time for tea" he said.

We needed it, after the adrenaline rush, my mouth was dry, and I was still excited, a cupper and a rest would calm us down, Ned was laying on top of a hill, with the binoculars, then he came back, "army patrol but gone past" he said.

"Thank the stars" I muttered, when we had finished tea we journeyed back to Ned's village.

We were warmly welcomed, but treated as royalty after Ned explained to the elders of our part in the venture, "got any ideas of how to smuggle out the diamonds" I asked Ned, when we met later in the day, "all taken care of" he replied, "same way as usual with other chiefs sons" he said smiling, "but getting a bit risky now".

"Have to find another way, but you will have to stay a few days.

For all to be ready" "Okay" we replied.

We need a rest anyway, after three days Ned came up to us, and said "all is ready, you can go to Accra when you like," he gave us each a necklace.

Look closely he gestured, on looking we could spot the raw diamonds, fixed in the necklace and painted to look like the other beads, "good" he said, "this way you'll get by" then he gave me a number to ring in England, "you ring chiefs son, he sell diamonds for you, you make much money" he then gave us two more necklaces.

"Give to chiefs son also please" looking I could see they were the same as ours, "so that's how they smuggle them out" Rob said.

"what a brilliant idea" then we stowed them in our backpacks, Rob and I decided to go next day to Accra airport, fly to Cairo, spend a few days there looking around at different places, then fly home from there as ordinary tourists.

And hopefully get away with it, well, we got away with it, I went back several times after that, after we set up a small import business selling African relics, a good way for the smuggling of diamonds, on my last trip after a large haul, the adrenaline rush was great.

"No next time" Ned said "that this was the last time, it was getting too dangerous and the authorities were getting suspicious".

"So one last big haul, that should keep the villages going for a few years yet, and as times were changing the young men were leaving as they grew up.

only us old ones left" he ventured, "Okay" I replied "lets fill up every thing we can find" a backpack full of stones is very heavy indeed, after our excursion, I could see Ned was ill.

"I wouldn't be able to make any more trips anyway" he said, "I go to join my father soon," at the airport we hugged each other as we said our last goodbye's, "farewell old friend, and don't worry about the villagers.

I've enjoyed our times together and I will miss them" "and I you" he replied, "good health" turning he clambered into the jeep and drove off, I stood and watched him go with tears in my eyes.

Sure we were rich Rob and me, as I shared half with him on each trip, we were now in business together, and quite successful, but it won't be the same without Ned, or as he was known among the villages that he helped to survive in the hard times, they knew him as DIAMOND JIM.

ESPANSA

We the exploration unit, had landed at the place chosen, to seek out and meet the ruler of this world of the third sun.

I and one unit of troopers, boarded a skimmer, we landed in front of the largest strangest building we could see.

On alighting we went to the gateway, and were surrounded by strangely dressed troopers, with strange weapons, we were probably just as strange to them.

I asked to see "their ruler" touching my throat com, which had a translator attached, because of the language differences on other worlds, these strange men showed us into a great hall.

which at the end sat a Great Lady, and her companion, we walked forward, and on reaching the steps, I issued the command through my helmet mike, "halt, but stay alert" then we went on one knee, and I bowed my head to the Great Lady, then stood and touching my throat mike, spoke to her, "greetings Great Lady, I am Thoruk knight of Valsador, commander of this expedition, and I am empowered to greet you from our own Great lady, Orothina of Maann".

Then to my surprise, the Lady's companion jumped up and ordered the guards "to retain us" our translators translate languages both ways, my troopers reacted instantly, to defend me and themselves.

At first one was slightly injured, as they were still on one knee, before the Lady.

As I had been, missiles came from the guards.

"Rally" I shouted in my com, I and my troopers ran and surrounded the Great Lady, to defend her from attack, I fired a knock out blast at the Lady's companion, who fell back into his high seat, my troopers fired their lasers, with quick accuracy, after a short while, the Lady stood up and said aloud, "stop this at once, I command you" the guards stopped, and I ordered "cease fire" "Lady approaching" I heard in my com, I turned and knelt on one knee to the Lady.

She looked at me and asked, "why did you kill my guards" I replied, "Great Lady your companion ordered your guards to kill us, we but defended ourselves and you, which is our duty" and added, "companion is only stunned not dead, did we do wrong" I questioned, there was a slight pause, "no, no, just a mistake by the king" "ha" I thought, that's his name, odd though" "please will you take your soldiers and return to your conveyance, and I will speak with you tomorrow" the Great Lady asked, "gladly I will await your envoy" then I ordered the troopers back to the skimmer, and followed them.

"What a start" I thought, "hope all works well" on the way back, I spoke to the troopers, "well done, although we killed eight guards, your loyalty will not go unnoticed" in the morning when a messenger arrived, we climbed aboard two skimmers, I had two units with me this time, as went to meet the Lady.

On reaching the Great Lady, we knelt and greeted her, as is our custom, then stood, waiting her reply.

The troopers stood back to back, having been alerted about yesterday's events; there were more people here this time, probably to have a look at us, no doubt.

"how long will the king be asleep" the Lady enquired, "he should be awake by now Great Lady, shall I have a doctor look at him, for you" "yes I think so" she replied, "our medical doctors know of no cure" I gave the order over my com "for a medic" and in a few moments a medic arrived, with her floating medical bed, the Great Lady ordered two guards "to take the medic to the king" two troopers followed as well, the Lady's guards seemed nervous of the troopers, after yesterday, "come Sir, sit with me, and we can talk" the Lady gestured.

And walked to a side door, who is "Sir" I thought, she stopped and looked back, "knight if you please" I followed with four troopers, we went to a room with a large table in the middle, and items on it, "eat" the Lady motioned to the table.

"I'm not sure if we can, one of the troopers will try the food first" a trooper removed her helmet, all present gasped, and the Great Lady looked alarmed, "helmet on" I ordered, this was done instantly, I asked the Great Lady.

"Did the sight of the trooper offend her" "oh, no" she replied, "just the colour" ha I thought "I will explain" and calling one of her guards over to me, "lower your weapon to me" which he did, "this is the colour of the troopers skin, but not shiny" as I pointed to the blade, "silver" she replied, "and this is the colour of her hair" I pointed to a colour on the guards uniform, "dark red" I was told, "and we all have eyes the colour of your sky" "pale blue" was mentioned.

"So if this is acceptable, the trooper will remove her helmet and gloves" "yes of course, now we know" the Lady motioned the trooper to do so, the trooper removed her helmet and gloves, all was okay this time, the Lady motioned a female companion to cut up the fruit onto different plates, for the trooper to try, the first apple, which was liked, "it is sweet and juicy" the trooper informed us, I could hear the other troopers muttering, in my com, "silence" I ordered, "Great Lady the other troopers would like to try the fruit, may they" I queried, "please do, and you Sir".

The Lady said, "Sir" I thought "who is it I could not see anyone other than us".

"Come knight, sit with me and talk" the Lady motioned to the other end of the table, "knight" the Lady explained, "Sir is a term we use for respected males" "ha, now I under stand, I am called Sir" I remarked, "and by your stance I believe you are male" "I am Great lady" I nodded, "please Sir" came the reply, "I am not called Lady on this world, I am queen Luamso, of Espansa, and normally addressed as Majesty" "Majesty and not Great lady" I repeated, "this is duly noted, I may call you Great Lady in my language, but the translator will automatically refer to you as Majesty" "Sir" her Majesty said again, "will you not take off your helmet and gloves, to try some fruit" "Majesty, maybe I had better explain further" I called a female companion to me, "this is the colour of my skin" and pointed to the clothing worn by the companion, "pale green" was the reply, "and this" I pointed to a finger item, "is the colour of my hair" "gold" I was told, "ha duly noted, Majesty, I am different in colour from the troopers, as I am a knight, from Valsador, the troopers are Ulan maidens, from Urh, all troopers are female, but I have noticed that all your people are the same colour".

"Quite so now kindly remove your helmet, so that I may look at you" was the request.

I obeyed, and removed my helmet and gloves, "hmm your quite a handsome man" "ha" I thought, "flattery will get you every where" "thank you" I replied, Majesty continued, "we will soon get used to each others ways and colour, there will be a little staring at first, but it will soon pass, I would like your troopers to visit our city and look around, when not on duty, this can be arranged"? was the question, "yes Majesty but first I think we should introduce ourselves to your people, as our first contact was not very good" "Yes tomorrow I will call a public meeting and explain the differences, then your troopers can mix with my people, talk and walk around" "um before I say yes, I will have a trooper disrobe, your people seem to be covered all over, troopers are not, if you think their dress is not right, I am not sure what to do, Majesty, disrobe" I ordered a trooper, which she did, I heard the guards shuffle, "hold still" majesty commanded them.

"My apologies Sir, my people are not used to seeing a woman so scantily dressed, short almost knee length boots, sort of short skirt, and a short top piece, this would cause a lot of trouble outside" her Majesty laughed.

"But this is their natural dress, do you have any suggestions, but they must suit both sides, I cannot order my troopers to dress as your companions do, Majesty"

"I to will think on this problem Sir, but for now, things will remain as they are, now you must return to your transport, and I will send an envoy for you tomorrow, as agreed" "yes Majesty" I bowed and we left the town, went back to the cruiser, "phew" I muttered to myself, I'm glad that's over, now for a change, and a relaxing drink.

I was relaxing in my quarters with a drink and the lights low, my eyes were shut and I was just lying there, listening to music and thinking, when I heard the door slide open then shut with a swish, I knew who it was, my beloved.

She sat beside me and held my hand, no one would dare enter a commanders quarters without permission, except an emergency, and Onin does not need permission.

Especially for our meetings, as by our code, a liaison between a Ulan trooper and her commander was not permitted, only by permission from our Great Lady, our meetings were illegal, but none of my troopers would speak of it, this is their code, soon I would be asking permission from our Great Lady, and I know it will be granted.

It was early afternoon before a messenger arrived, "her Majesty wishes you to come Sir, as arranged to show your selves to the people" the troopers only wore light Armour this time, we went to the city, and met her Majesty in the city square, which was crowded, so I said to the troopers.

"We are to be a public spectacle for a short time anyway, mix and talk with the people, but stay in pairs".

We removed our helmets and gloves, silence reigned, but for a short pause, then people were chatting as the troopers moved among them, "we only have our own exchange items to give your people for anything the troopers may wish to buy" I bought a handful out of my pocket, to show her majesty, "I hope they will not be offended".

"Oh dear no these items we value, you have diamonds, emeralds, rubies and sapphires, with this handful you could buy the city Sir" her Majesty said, and knowing the troopers had heard this, they would bargain well, I turned my com off, "how is the king" her Majesty enquired, "he should be with you tomorrow, your metabolism is different from ours,

so it has taken longer for your companion king to recover"
I did not mention, because of his outburst the first time we
met, that we had indoctrinated him while he slept, he would
show more respect for her Majesty, and not speak out of
turn, nor any more outbursts.

I approached her Majesty on the subject of "presenting the
families of the guards that we killed, a handful of diamonds,
emeralds and rubies, as a token" she agreed "and that it was
most a generous offer, which would not be refused" "they
value our tokens of diamonds, emeralds and such like, I will
have a cruiser go to Insibar, the shiny planet, and obtain a
large clear stone, diamond I think, then I could present it
to her majesty, as a token of friendship, yes" I thought, "it
shall be done" as the sky darkened, we all went back to the
cruiser, and the troopers were carrying lots of different fruit,
and other strange items, that I did not know, they enjoyed it.

By the babble of noise they made, I determined that all
should have time in the city market, after all, we had been
on campaign for quite a while, and to relax and enjoy
themselves, would be a good moral booster.

Onin showed me what she had bought, strange ornaments,
some fruit, and clothing, she was happy, that made me
happy too.

I went to a fruit trader in the market, and asked if he would supply enough fruit, every one of their weeks for the whole crew, I gave him six of the stones, he said that would be plenty enough, "I will give you six of these every week" he was stunned I think, he just looked and nodded, Two days later I sent a messenger to her majesty, to ask "if a guard could teach troopers to ride their animals called horses, as some would like to try" after a while two guards arrived with horses, they were admitted into the perimeter, troopers dressed in their natural clothes, as Ulan maids, came out of the cruiser, the guards just looked and stared.

"This is the natural clothes of their world do not be ashamed of them" I said, "we are not ashamed Sir knight, just not used to it" "ha" I conjectured, "you'll get used to it don't worry" I watched several trying to ride, but falling off, no real harm done though, a medic was at hand, after a couple of days, some seemed to ride good, no matter though they enjoyed it, and that's what counted.

I was told a long time ago, that a good commander always puts the welfare of his troopers first, after the code, this is what I had followed, and it worked, I asked the guards "if they could still teach the troopers to ride" they replied, "that they were at our disposal" I suspect the younger guard was happy to stay, as a certain trooper always seemed to be near him.

The next two weeks were spent in leisure pursuits, many of the troopers had learned to ride the horses, her Majesty had given us, as a good will gesture, two hundred of these animals, they had also been shown how to look after them, but they were not allowed outside the perimeter without being dressed in the suits made for this world, Earlier some had purchased material, and had a suit made, a type of jacket, and trousers, this was acceptable to all.

Ulan maids dressed in all sorts of colours, they liked them, so who was I to disagree, I called down another cruiser, so that the crew might enjoy themselves as mine were, I determined that each cruiser would do a month turn around, but we seem to have more guards to help teach the troopers to ride, I can guess why, we seem to have a few young male onlookers as well, outside the perimeter.

Those who could ride helped to teach others to ride, and after a few weeks, all could ride quite well, including me, after some merriment from the troopers, when I fell off a couple of times, Onin came to my rescue, although not needed, I let her, I liked it, normally strict rules apply to the troopers, but I had relaxed these, while off duty, it worked well.

This gave me an idea, I looked at a map of this world, which we had made, when surveying this world, with permission from her majesty, I found what I was looking for, not too far away, I then approached her Majesty, and informed her "that I would.

Like to make a permanent home on this world" and showed her on the map an island that I had picked out, "it is as calculated in your miles, a thousand long and five hundred wide" "ah yes, it is a deserted place, a desert island, nobody has lived there for as long as I know, it is yours, Sir knight".

I explained that "I had nine other cruisers on another planet, their moon as they call it, who would be here, ten thousand troopers in all" she just smiled and left the room, "did she guess" I thought, as I returned to the cruiser.

When I relayed the information to our own Great Lady, Orothina, she was delighted with the news, and wished to speak with her Majesty, via video com link, this I arranged with her Majesty, who was nervous of coming to the cruiser, understandably though, it is nearly as big as the city, I assured her "all would be well, and she could bring as many guards as she wished" "it's not the guards" she replied, "just the size of it" "don't be alarmed Majesty, you are safer in the cruiser than anywhere, you are a Great Lady, I and my troopers are sworn to protect you with our lives, this is our code, as you may remember when we first met, and our Lady is the same as me in colour but her hair is white, she is also the same height as us, in your measurements, five feet ten.

So there is no surprise for you, she is also firm but fair, as you are" "I am ready now Sir let's go" I took her Majesty to my private com room, all troopers acknowledged her majesty on the way in, after establishing a link, through the relay stations on other planets, because of the distance.

I was ordered by my own Great Lady to leave the room, as they wished to speak privately, so I bowed to both and left the room, leaving her Majesty and two maids alone to talk with Orothina, after what seemed ages, a maid came out of the room, and said "that her Majesty is ready to return back to the palace Sir" "hup" I ordered in my com, as troopers stood to attention, we try to make orders as short as possible, saves time, we took her Majesty and maids back to the palace, "how fast can this cruiser go" Majesty asked, I called a "halt" we hovered in mid air, "see that great hill" "mountain" I was told, "ah so, how far is it, in your miles" "about fifty" was the reply, "calculate" I told the on board computer, which came back, at full speed, ten minutes, "do you wish to go there Majesty" "another day, Sir I have had a tiring day so far" "of course" and we flew them gently home.

A few days later, I met her Majesty, at her request, "Sir" she said, "I would like you to show us, on this world, the power of your weapons, some we have seen what they can do, others we do not know, like the strange light swords".

"That all carry, all the time" "yes majesty I will arrange it, the light swords are a normal part of our attire, for self defense, very useful at close quarter combat, if I could have some old Armour and weapons, I will put on a display, in a few days time" "good" was the reply, then she spoke to a guard, "let it be so" I bowed and left, I went to the market place to have a look around, then back to the cruiser, when the Armour and weapons arrived, I worked out a routine for the troopers, and asked my number one troop to perform the task, on the day of the demo, the whole of the city citizens were gathered in a large field, that had been designated by her majesty.

We had erected echo chambers on poles all around the place, for all to hear what was said, when all were assembled, and the troopers ready, I stood and spoke to the people.

"Do not be alarmed by what you see, your safety comes first, and you will not be harmed in any way" I assured them, I heard a murmur from the crowd, then gave the command to begin, first four troopers arrived, and had a mock battle, with their light swords, then they hacked some Armour and weapons to pieces.

Just to show what they could really do, a cheer came from the crowd, I was startled, for a moment, and just stood and stared at them.

"We are not used to such acclaim" I mentioned to her majesty, she just smiled, the troopers bowed, waved and walked away, next came an armed skimmer, which felled a tree, with one blast, did a flying loop and a roll, then flew away, then came a walker, a machine with two troopers in it, a shield up front to protect them from light fire, the crowd were hushed, the walker fired at an old cart we had put about a thousand yards away, the cart shattered into small pieces, then it returned to the cruiser.

Four more troopers came, and shattered more Armour with their light rifles, on full blast, bowed and left, "this is our armament" I addressed the people, "and now the best for last" the cruiser came into view, more murmurs from the crowd, some cowered down, "see that mountain top over there" I said.

Pointing, "watch the top" a flash from one of the cruisers forward blasters, and by the time you turned your head, a flash of light and a cloud of dust in the distance, and the mountain top disappeared.

"This is the might of our total armament, but only one blaster was fired, there are six up front, thank you for watching" I then sat down next to her majesty, "glad that's over" I muttered, her majesty put out her hand, as if to touch me, I jumped back out of arms reach, the lady looked startled, "Sir" she questioned, looking round, "your troopers have their weapons aimed at you".

"Quite so your majesty, it is our code, that if I had let you touch me, they would have fired, and I would be dead, I may be their commander, but not above the code" I waved the weapons down, as I was out of arms reach, "by our code if we have your permission to wear your colour, then you may touch us, without us being killed, we may never touch you, you are a Great Lady, and Majesty, to touch you, without an emergency being present, it is a death penalty, by our code for sure".

"Then you have my permission to wear my colour sir" I relaxed and stepped closer, safe now, knowing the troopers had heard the reply, "hold out your arm Sir I wish to walk with you" I put my arm straight out, her majesty laughed, and called a guard over, "show Sir knight, how a man holds his arm for a lady to walk with him" this the guard did, "this is what I wish sir, so that I way walk with you".

I copied the guards strange angle of arm, just above the waist, and bent, a bit awkward I thought, her majesty rested her arm on mine, and we walked back to the palace, I heard a couple of giggles, on my com, "yes" I thought, "I knew what the troopers were thinking" but I let them be, "what did you think of our little display" I asked, "impressive, I asked about your weapons, because on part of this world, we are hit by burning rocks from space, at a certain time of the year, and everyone has to hide in the mountain caves, and rebuild their houses each time, and I wondered if you could help" "no problem Majesty, I will have a scientist calculate where they come from, a cruiser can orbit that area, and smash them to dust, with it's light blasters, if you would show me on the map, which of your islands are affected by the rocks, and tell me what time of year, all will be done" after her Majesty had shown me, I relayed the information to a science officer.

I assured her majesty that once we knew where in space they came from, we could go into space and destroy them, long before they reach this world, some of your people can go along as well if they wish, to observe the destruction of these stones, and a ride in space, among the stars, what is your colour, that we may wear on our uniforms, Majesty, the white band that you see, is our Lady's" "blue" majesty announced, "blue it shall be then" I echoed.

And left her majesty in her room at the castle, to return to the cruiser.

When next I met her Majesty she asked, out of curiosity mainly, "why we were different in colour," "I will explain further, Majesty, in our system of worlds, there are three, Maann, is the largest, where our Great Lady lives, my world Valsador, and Urh, are about half the size, the men of my world, become knights, if they wish to, and on Urh, the maidens become troopers, if they also wish to, Valsador and Urh, are the size of this world, a light sword is presented to a learner, when they become troopers, they are a personal.

Thing and each have their name on them, including mine.

On our worlds, if you see a maiden wearing a light sword, you know that she is a trooper, and commands respect, it is an honour, for no one may carry a light sword, except troopers and knights" "ah now I understand your difference in colour, and the light swords, thank you Sir knight for explaining" and I added, "we could present your guards with light swords, if you wished, Majesty, and teach them how to use them safely, in an untrained hand, the person wielding it, can hurt themselves, light swords can be a lethal weapon" "I will think on your generous offer Sir" I bowed and left, I had ordered two cruisers from our base on this worlds moon, to check out the island, which was to be our home here, on this world, this took a few day's, after making sure the island was safe, I then ordered all the cruisers to land there, and to set up buildings for all to live in, and we would create our own environment, with plants and trees from our worlds, like home from home, a large area was for the horses, as more were purchased, and an area for apples, peaches, plums, and pears to grow, Orchard is the word I think, as well as our own types of fruit trees, and plants, which are much more colourful than this worlds.

Because trees here are all brown with green leaves, two cruisers were sent back home, to collect a mixture of plants and trees, and some building material, more equipment, for the job, we have a variety of coloured trees, the pink trees of Urh, which give off a heavy scent, quite pleasant though, green and blue trees of my world, slightly scented, and some green and red trees from Maann, these are also scented, we could make this a colourful place to live, it will take the cruisers about two months to make the journey, at star speed.

I had also let the joined troopers go along as well, so they could have a little time with their husbands and children.

In the meantime, two hundred of the horses had been taken to the island, more were purchased, and taken there, totaling two thousand in all, the troopers who had learned to ride taught the others to ride as well, as a means of recreation, and getting around, slower than a skimmer, but more enjoyable, while visiting her Majesty which I did often, she remarked "that she and the king, would be away for quite some time.

"Visiting other islands" I remarked, "that I and all my troopers with skimmers, and cruisers, were at their disposal, we could make the journey safer and quicker, than their floating wooden boats, a cruiser at a steady speed, could fly around your world in one of your hour's, star speed would be too fast.

It was calculated at about "six hundred and eighty million of this worlds miles an hour" "hmm" came the reply, "and we could visit islands that we only go once every ten year's, because of the journey time, yes we would like that, Sir knight, and we could go every year" I nodded, we worked out a travel plan, the Majesty's and eight guards, in one skimmer, with an escort skimmer of troopers, skimmers are small, and can only take ten people comfortably, they could visit the whole world in two months, and stay at each destination a week, the actual journey would be by cruiser, then by skimmer on the last part, we had a practice first.

For the guards to get used to the cruiser in flight, and skimmer, the Majesty's joined them.

We took them all for a flight at a slow speed, of about two thousand of their miles an hour, for them to see some islands, although one guard felt sick, but soon recovered, this we practiced three times, I think the king liked the troopers in natural costume, this done then, when her Majesty was ready she would contact us, via video com link, we had installed a consul in the castle, for the Majesty's to talk to us, which to my surprise, Majesty could work quite well.

A cruiser was standing by ready, after they had finished their tour, which was "a success" I was told, her Majesty asked "if video com links could be set up on each major island" "of course" I replied, "a good idea, I will set about it at once, it should take only a short time to establish".

I bowed and left, After spending some time setting up the video coms, and teaching the people to use them, I had an occasion to see her Majesty, and to inform her "that I and eight other cruisers would be going on a mission to distant stars, but we would only be away two of their years, (one and a half in our years, time is longer on our home worlds,) and that there would always be a cruiser on our island, named Queens island, in her honour, for their protection, and use.

The same as I and my troopers had done, also when we return, I have the consent of our Great Lady Orothina, to join with my maiden Onin, the ceremony will be on our island, we would like your Majesty's to attend, and as many people who wish to come, you will see the troopers perform their maiden dance, in their national costume, which you have seen, mine is similar, a short skirt and boots with a loose shirt, some of your young men may get excited by the dance, it is expected, I was as a young man, when I first saw the dance, it is meant to attract men, to be lovers or husbands".

And I added "because of the code, if they should choose any of your young men, I cannot interfere, they are fit and healthy, most are virgins, one or two are joined, with husbands and children at home, so, if you have no objections Majesty" I queried, "we have no objections Sir" her Majesty smiled, and they agreed to attend our joining as well, "I will miss our talks, and the game called chess, with your companion, king" which I had now befriended, I knelt and asked for their "blessing on our journey" this was freely given.

But tinged with sadness, I know that we would soon return to this world called, ESPANSA.

FRIENDS

⊱⊰

*A*fter being in my new house for about a month, I thought that I would mow the lawn, which is quite big for me, about a hundred and fifty foot long, by fifty foot wide, and as gardening is not my subject, and I have to be in the right frame of mind to do it.

but I'm going to get a proper firm next year, for all these tasks, I got the mower out from the garage, got to the lawn, and eventually got it going, on starting to cut the grass, which was getting quite long now, I was going across the lawn, muttering to myself, about having to cut it.

When I almost ran over a mouse, or so I thought at first, but no, as I picked it up, I could see it was human like, a little kind of person, probably dazed after being blown over by the air from my hover mower.

as I held it in my hand, it sat up, and immediately jumped to its feet, he then began to stab me with its stick, although no more than a sliver of wood, but it gave you a sting, much like sticking your thumb on a thorn.

"whoa" I shouted, which blew it over, and I nearly dropped it, then I muttered, "oops stupid me" so I began to speak to it in a whisper, "hello, can you understand me" it nodded its head, then he said something, but I couldn't understand, what was said, it's voice was so faint, that I could just hear it, so I just smiled at it to show I was friendly, and whispered to it "that I meant it no harm".

if anyone had seen me, they would have thought me bonkers, talking to a mouse, but I could see it was afraid, it was shivering, so would I be, I thought, with someone who could hold me in his hand, a bit like Jack and the beanstalk, then, "aha" an idea occurred, "food, that's a good ice breaker" so I closed my hand around it, being careful not to crush it, then took it into the house.

I think this really frightened it as I could just hear it speak, and it was wriggling to get free, but I just smiled at it, not really knowing what else to do, "poor little creature" I thought, with its furry little body, long pointed ears, and stubby tail, who might be thinking that it was my dinner today, I went to the kitchen, opened the fridge, took out some chicken, and some cheese, laid them on the table, then went to get some bread, all single handed.

as I still had the little thing in my other hand, to stop it running away, and not knowing what it ate, might only eat green stuff, I sat down at the table, pulled off some chicken, a small piece for my guest, although as big as it, I put some cheese beside the meat, then pulled off some chicken for myself, and began to eat.

I gently set my hand on the table beside the food, and slowly opened my fingers, it looked up at me, then sniffed the food, tasted a little cheese, then spit it out, next, it tried the chicken, sat down, and began to eat, it ate quite a lot for its size.

I assumed that hunger had overcome its fear of me, it put some chicken in a bag, which it carried under its coat, which I first thought was the creature, "but no" probably a mouse coat, a bit like us humans in the ice age, it then pointed to the door, and then to the window.

Muttering something that I could not understand, it did this twice, then I understood, what he meant, stupid me.

I picked it up, it sat in my hand and I just about closed it, took it into the garden, and put it down on the ground, the place where I had first found it, it picked up a small stick, probably its spear, and scampered off into the hedge, and was gone from sight.

I turned back to the mower, and finished cutting the grass, but keeping an eye out for any small creatures, that may be around, and not knowing how many there were, especially if they were foraging for food.

I had thought about what happened, while I was mowing the lawn, did it really happen, or was I daydreaming, I put away the lawn mower, went back into the kitchen to check, the bread, chicken and cheese, were still there on the table where I had left them, when I took the little thing outside, scraps of chicken were where it had sat, and a piece of fur, picking it up, I examined it, it was a small bag, as we would know it, with slivers of wood in it, little spears or knives, who knows?.

"But quite ingenious" I thought, "so it was true, I'm not going bonkers yet" I sat down in amazement, and started to think, "what was the little thing really like under its coat" many questions came to mind, "were they really its ears, was that really its tail, did it have a furry body, how many more were there, where did it live" my imagination ran wild, "was it what we call a pixie or elf, were there really fairies at the bottom of my garden, who knows"?

But I resolved to find out I related my tale to the wife when she came in from her shopping trip, I think that I was going on a bit, as she told me to "slow down, calm down, and speak slower".

I guess I was a bit over wrought, to say the least, after I had calmed down, I showed her the bag, but I'm not sure she didn't think that was I bonkers, but agreed, "That I should find out more".

"I think I was just being humored, for peace and quiets sake" but I didn't care, I knew what I had seen, and taken place.

Next morning I put some more pieces of chicken, bread, and cheese, all cut up small, in the hedge where I had seen him disappear, went back to the house, and stood by the side of the lounge window, looking out to see if the little man would come again.

I was hoping so, eventually, he came, just when I thought that he wouldn't come, especially after the events of the day before.

There were two others this time, they ate some meat and bread, sniffed at the cheese, but left it, "ha" I muttered to myself, "cheese is off the menu" they put the meat into their little bags, picked up some bread, and disappeared into the hedge, "where do they go from here I wondered, I must get a stronger pair of binoculars, as these that I was using were only a small pair, and not very powerful".

off to town I went, about five miles away, found a sports shop, and purchased a really powerful pair, although quite expensive, what the hell, I thought, it's worth it, even if only for curiosity's sake, reaching home again, I pushed the remote button to open the gates, they shut automatically, drove in, pressed the garage door button, I liked all these gadgets, they saved time, they closed behind me.

Walking out the side door, I noticed the wife's gardening tools on the front lawn, old green fingers has been at it again, I mused to myself, the wife is the gardener in our house, and a jolly good one too.

I went into the house, and found her in the kitchen, drinking tea, "I'm not going near the hedge" she said, "it's either mice, that were scampering around in there, or your little thing, either way I didn't like it, so I came in" like most females, she didn't like mice, rats, spiders, or any other creepy crawlies, they weren't my favourite either, so I had a cuppa with her, then I went to the garden to remove the gardening tools, from near the hedge, as I picked them up, I peered into the hedge, but couldn't see anything.

Disappointed, I went back into the house, to carry on with the rest of the day, but couldn't wait for morning to come, thoughts and ideas went through my mind, during the rest of the day, and I had a solution, I think.

After feeding the little people, I went to town, and purchased a pin microphone, like the ones they have on telly chat shows, also some earphones, and a small pocket radio, I had an idea, to connect the microphone into the radio circuit, and with the headphones on, I would be able to hear what the little man said, should the occasion arise again, hopefully it would.

Money was no problem, as we had a share in the lottery win, which had allowed us to buy the house in the first place, and both of us to retire early, and enjoy life, being an electrician in my working life, to adapt the pocket radio, was no problem at all, for a man of my caliber, or so I thought.

After about four attempts, with wire and soldering iron, I finally got it right, more by luck than judgment, I closed the radio case, and the microphone on a foot of wire, "that should do, at least to try out" I told myself, now I was ready, but not quite, what about me, speaking to them, another microphone was needed, back to town I went, purchased one, wired it into the volume control switch, and with the volume down as low as possible, it was barely audible to me, but just right, now I really was ready for anything.

Next morning I put the meat and bread out as usual, went inside to the bedroom window, to get a better view with my new binoculars, after I got them adjusted properly, I sat down on a chair, rested my elbows on the window sill and waited. eventually they came, took the meat and bread, then went back into the hedge, I scanned along the hedge for movements, and saw them struggling along in the lower branches near the ground, I followed them for a few feet, then they disappeared from view, I checked for several mornings, always at roughly the same spot, "did they live underground"? I wondered, but how to find out without being obvious, having a think, I know, I had a brainwave, "trim the hedge, it was looking a bit overgrown anyway" I got out the electric hedge trimmer, and got to work, first I trimmed the side of the hedge, keeping an eye out for anything that moved, but nothing did, I assumed the noise of the trimmer frightened them off, next I started on the back hedge, being doubly careful, and cutting slower, first I cut the top, then the inside, looking all the time, then I almost finished the outside of the hedge, when a loud bang, jumping back startled, "what's that" I said aloud.

when I checked, I had been so intent on looking for the little people, that I wasn't being careful enough, I had cut through the electric cable, "what a fat twit" I called myself, "that's that for the day".

While clearing up the leaves and twigs, especially at the place where they vanished, I had a good look, but couldn't see anything in the hedge, on the ground, nothing, not a sign anywhere, "what now"? I pondered the question, "where are they, are they watching me, I had to be very careful, so as not to alarm them, but how to find out" then a thought occurred to me, "set up the camcorder, put it on a tripod, in the field behind the hedge, first I would need some wooden posts and some chicken wire, to stop the sheep in the field from knocking it all over".

As I was doing this one morning, the farmer came along, and asked me "what I was doing in his field" as I explained to him, "that I was keen on nature and wanted to film some hedgerow animals" but added "that I was sorry, and apologized for using his field, I had not disturb the sheep, but I didn't know how to find out who owned the field and woods, to get permission, or buy them from, if for sale" the last statement made him look, "buy, well" he said, "it's a small field about two acres, if your serious in what you say, you can buy the copse as well" I said.

"That I certainly was" he agreed, that I could carry on filming while the deeds were exchanged, and I let him keep his sheep in the field, till the end of the year as well.

At last I got the camcorder set up on the outside of the hedge, without any problems, all this time I was still leaving food out for the little people, and they still took it, without fail every day.

The same routine, they would disappear, I set up the camcorder, focusing at the foot of the hedge with as wide an angle as possible, and the zoom lens on full, at about fifteen feet away, I didn't think that this would disturb them, but how to operate it, I needed a remote control, so I bought some wire with a push button, another day gone, and still no wiser, over the next few days I filmed, but could not find anything on the film, even after stop/ start and pause, I searched each section of film, "had I got it wrong, but where"? So I spent the next day in town, in the camera shop, I told them that I was a bird watcher, and that I wanted to film up close without disturbing them, they were quite pleased to help, well, I did spend a lot of money that day, a few grand at least, ordering fiber optic lenses, the size of a pencil and an inch long, also a special camera and screen, with lots of special cable, and all this could be operated by remote control from the house, or automatically by movement, brilliant I thought, well pleased with myself.

It would be about ten days before they arrived, even by special courier, but now I had to go and sign the deeds, for the land and the copse, this done, "there's no stopping me now" I thought, quite cheerfully.

At last the camera and lenses arrived, then I set about the task of setting them up, the instructions were a bit confusing as to what plugged in where, but I managed, after reading them at least twice, I put one in the hedge, at the spot where they disappear, one a few feet further along, on the other side, and one at the corner of the hedge, and one looking down from a nearby tree, all this took me a few days, and I was getting impatient, "calm down" I told myself, "patience is a virtue, not I think that I have many virtues" I next set up the camera in the field, then set up the screen and remote control in my study, as I call it, a small box room really, but it serves my purpose, after I had got the focusing right, "lets try again" I thought, but couldn't wait for morning to come.

I left the food as usual, and knowing that having fed them for the past two months, they had come to depend on me, like wild birds do, if you feed them regularly, I went indoors to my study, turned on the screen, camera, and lenses, then sat down to wait, sure enough they came, took the food, and went, I just caught a glimpse of them on lens two, then switched to lens four, they moved faster than I thought, probably the best way to stay alive in the wild, run, "ha" I muttered, progress at last, I seem to be talking to myself a lot these days, but I'm not mad, although as the wife said, I was getting a little obsessed, "now where to put the lenses next"? I put them on trees one next to the corner tree, and the others scattered on other trees.

Where I thought they might go, now I had to wait to try them out, this time I got them on all four lenses, so my guess was right, they went from tree to tree, running from one shelter to another, a good survival tactic.

I moved the lenses further into the copse, but missed them on two lenses, "wrong way, twit head" I told myself, I put them at where I thought they would be, it was a zigzag pattern from tree to tree, I eventually tracked them on an angle course through the copse, and down to the river bank, a small stream ran alongside the copse, from another wood, a half mile away.

This I knew to be a forestry commission wood, with walks and picnic areas, solid tables, and bench seats, hmm, I pondered the question? "Do they live near there, and collect left over food from the picnickers, all through the summer months.

And over time have learnt our language? And hope to survive the winter, maybe they hibernated, I didn't know"? and as summer was nearly over, and the days were starting to turn cold, they would depend on me even more now, I went home to think, an idea was forming in my mind, "what if they came to live in my wood, they could have all the freedom they wanted, and protection as well".

This I had thought to ask the little thing, well as best as I could, but I had to get close to them first, I resolved to do this over the next few days, when I put out the food, I would sit down by the hedge and wait for them, with my made up microphone.

hopefully we could talk, next day I put the food out as usual, and sat down to wait, "I could build them houses" I thought, "like dolls houses, or whatever they wanted" lots of thoughts raced through my mind, "but first I had to ask them, after all, they might not want to come".

I had lengthened the wire to the radio, as a foot was too short for the purpose in mind, I put the radio, and microphone near to where the food was, waiting their arrival, I was nervous, and a bit apprehensive, as they approached, I lifted my hand in greeting, then spoke to them, this startled them a bit, then I spoke again, and said "this way we can talk".

After a little while one approached the radio, in their type of English, "sss, we talk" I outlined my plan, in as simple a fashion as I could, as their speaking seemed limited, and most things were done by sign language, I think they finally understood what I meant, and with a quick "we go" they disappeared as usual.

I went back into the house, and told my wife, of my plan, if it worked, "I hope they do come, then we can have some normality in this house" she said, "thank you my love" I replied, kissing her on the cheek, "I know what you mean, I'm sorry" I apologized to her, "but I just wanted to help them".

And she knows me better than I know myself, like most wives do, I fed them as usual for the next few days, on the fourth day I sat down as I had been doing, with the radio and mike, and waited their arrival, they came, and the one I had named George, spoke to me, "sss, we come, home bad, here good for chicks" that's how it sounded. "okay" I said, "good" half stunned with disbelief, I just sat there for a few minutes after they had gone, this was what I had wanted, but was beyond my wildest dreams, I stirred eventually, they had gone, and I had a lot of work to do, before winter set in, and my new friends arrive, I called the builder that I had arranged with to do the basic work, and asked him to start as soon as possible, I had told him that I was breeding quails, so that the work he would be doing in the wood, wouldn't be surprising to him at all, he could not start for a few days.

So I had some quick arrangements to make, as the work would take about two months to complete, and the weather was getting colder, and colder, and with my guests arriving at any time, I think for a minute I panicked.

"oh bloody hell, what am I going to do, what if the builder should see them, if they came now" thoughts raced around in my head, "what if, why, when, how, shut up" I told myself, "for pete's sake, have a cuppa, think straight, and be logical, get it sorted out" after a long think, I found a solution to my dilemma, "the tool shed, yes, that's it, for a temporary home, good" I cleaned out the shed, put some straw and wood shavings on the floor, but not knowing their habits, I would have to find out from them, what they needed, I also put a tree branch leaning on the wall, all this done, I was a lot happier now, then the builder arrived, with two men, and a mini digger.

To make digging easier, they started by digging around the edge of the wood, to put in a small concrete wall, two feet above ground level, and a foot wide.

On top of which would be a fence, six feet high, green plastic coated wire mesh, this would disguise it, and help it blend in with the trees.

the digging and concreting took about three weeks to do, during this time I had been taking the food across the field to the edge of the wood, to save the little people from getting hurt by the digger, while I had been taking the food to the woods, I had seen a few more of them, and had used my radio and mike to speak with some, I also asked "when they would come" we spoke in broken English, with much gesturing, and we conversed quite well this way, they told me, "we come when sun gone" I wasn't sure what was meant, but I guessed at the end of autumn.

The work in the wood was coming along nicely, the low wall around the wood was completed, and the uprights for the weld mesh were in place, they had started to dig out the base for the summer cage, which I called it, it was decided to have a summer cage in the woods and a winter house, which was to be built behind the tool shed, all with planning permission of course, for rearing quails, the summer cage base was to be quite big, spread between the trees, it would be forty feet long, and twenty feet wide, the base was six inches of concrete, to stop predators digging underneath, to get in, it was covered by a foot of earth, the weld mesh was to be six feet high, and covered over the top, like an aviary, covered in green plastic wire of course, to blend in, but would allow them to get in and out, if they wanted to, and with a door for me to get in, padlocked and with an alarm.

this would give them a large safe area to roam in, and rear their young, this included parts of trees, they could climb up into the lower branches.

And still be inside the mesh, safe from birds, and any small animals that could get in, they were soon dealt with, I had seen them deal with small animals before, such as mice, in the hedges, they could defend themselves very well, I had meant to build them houses of sorts for them to live in, but this would have to be sorted out at a later date, the two small bases were for quails, further over in the wood, "well I had to have a few quails didn't I".

But all this work took longer than expected, mainly because of the weather, one morning when I took the food to my friends, George, as I had named him, said "we come in two suns" slightly taken aback, I just stood there, like a dumb ox, then I said to George, "I take chick to see new home, now first" George replied, "sss, we come" "now see new home" so I put George and another in my top pocket, with the radio clipped on the outside, the others disappeared, and I walked back to the house.

Reaching home, I went straight to the tool shed, and showed them their temporary winter home, "good" George said, "where trees" "okay" I answered, "I get trees ready, for next sun" after taking George and his friend back to the wood, I went and cut off three big branches, from trees that weren't in their summer area, didn't want to take their trees away from them, these branches had plenty of leaves on them, I also put up some wooden shelves, and leant the branches on them, this was to give them a lot more space, and somewhere to hide.

which they seemed to like, all was ready, and I was quite excited at the prospect of at least doing something worthwhile, in my lifetime, I did not want to change their way of life, or to humanize them, just to feed them, and ensure their safety, the rest of the time they would be left to do whatever they did, in their own way, but the feeling of helping to save a race of beings, because they were a race, in their own right, and just to enhance their existence, for a better life, away from the dangers as far as I could, the thought overwhelmed me, I felt glad, but humble, and I wept for joy.

After I had explained all to my wife, who was as glad as me about it, I talked about the possibility of introducing our youngest daughter to the chick people, so that she could look after them, while we were away on holidays or for any other reason.

As we would not live forever, and she was a level headed person, and would keep the chicks safe as we will, although holidays were out this year, there's always next year, and so on, and we wanted every thing to look as normal as possible to everyone else, including the rest of our relations, some I wouldn't trust.

As we knew that if our new friends were found out, it would mean the end of their race, once the scientists got hold of them, that would definitely be it, I had already decided, that if I could not get them away, to another wood, preferably miles away, I would if necessarily (god forbid) destroy them myself, I knew not how yet.

But a possibility that I must face, and prepare for better that, than have them cut up, and experimented on, all in the name of science, or anything else, we decided to tell our daughter next year, and to introduce her to them, she was a great nature lover, and they would have no fear of her.

Next day was a big day for my friends and me, and it could prove to be very traumatic, especially for the little people, I went to the wood as usual, carrying a big cardboard box, cut down to three inches high.

With wood shavings in the bottom, and hoping that it was big enough, as I still didn't know how many of them there were, as counting to the chicks didn't mean much, so off I set, quite cheerfully, trying not to be too excited, for my own sake really, but I was shaking in my boots.

I arrived at the wood as usual, set the box down, and waited, I put some food out, set up the radio, and sat down by the box, as George knew by now and was not afraid to talk to me, although I had spoken to some of the others before, and so I waited, after half an hour, some appeared, George spoke to me, "we come now" "okay" I replied, then he waved his arm, and they began to appear, all looking the same, I put a piece of wood from the ground to the box rim, to help them in, they began to climb in, some a bit shy, but they came, I counted twenty in all, "are we all come" I asked George, "sss" "okay I take to new home" and off I set for home, carrying the box with it's precious load, some a little frightened, but ok, I walked as gently as I could, when we arrived at their new home for the winter, I unlocked the door, and turned on the light, they were all scampering around in the box, so I quickly laid it on the floor, and split it open, to let them out, they were scampering all over the place, and I wondered what had frightened them.

I put the radio down on the floor, and called for "George" I had to call for him three times, before he came out of hiding he was shivering, "why George afraid" I asked, "you make sun" he said, "no" I replied, "this man sun" and turned the light off then on again, "this not sun in sky" George seemed puzzled, "wait" I said, then I fetched the torch from the car, I laid it on the floor, and turned it on and off, a few times, "this man sun" I told him again, I motioned for him to try, and with a shove he moved the switch, on and off, then he nodded, and seemed to be much happier now, he seemed to understand a little more about us humans, and things we take for granted, a whole lot better than I had given him credit for.

I went and fetched some more food, and water, in a flat dish, I think that it was a type of baking tray, "ah, well" I thought, "better buy some more, before I get told off" I locked the door, and went to town with my wife, to do some shopping, and also to pick up some electrical parts, as I had an idea of sorts, a dimmer switch, with a small electric motor and a dog tooth belt, as the timer would time on, and the motor would turn slowly, and the lights would dim, much like the sun going down, then off, and visa versa in the morning, to give them sunrise, "yes" I thought "that's it, ideal for the purpose in hand" but I would need a much better version for the new winter house, that was soon to be built.

The fence of weld mesh, around the wood was all but finished, the concrete bases in the wood were all done, and the weld mesh around the summer area, was just being put up, next would be the trenches, for the power cables to the winter house, then the base would be laid, and the walls and roof would be put on at a later date, the winter house would be twenty feet long, by fifteen feet wide, with double glazed tinted windows, covered in weld mesh, electric locks on the doors, also heating and ventilation, security lights would be at strategic points, with a camera lens, the same as in the summer area, this would help to deter intruders, human or animal, and ensure a high degree of safety and privacy.

The winter passed quite uneventful, just the daily routine, of food and water for our guests, but because of language difficulties.

I was called which sounded like, "manbi" and the guests, I just called chick, with a click of the tongue, the winter and summer area's were finished now, and the builders gone, now I had to make them a house, for the summer area, the house I made was six feet long, four feet wide, and three feet high, this I thought "should give them plenty of room inside for sleeping, and wandering around, on wet days in summer".

I had put a floor, at a foot up, then another on top at a foot above that, with branches going up to each floor level, all from the base floor, all floors were covered in wood shavings, and scraps of cloth, which I thought "they might use for bedding" I also made the other house, for inside the winter house, the same design, so as that changing homes wouldn't seem so bad, or upsetting to the chick people.

I wired up the lights on the trees in the wood, and outside the winter house, with the detectors pointing at an offset angle, I next connected up the lenses in the wood, and a microphone in their house, for chick to speak to me, at any time, if anything was wanted, all these are connected to a voice activated unit, which is attached to the consul in my study, it controls the lenses as well, there's a warning bleep when it is activated, and there's a bleeper in our bedroom, in case of anything at night, but if I'm out it will also activate a set phone massage.

Now that spring is here again, and the chicks are in the summer area, they seem happy enough with the way things are, and I had just finished everything in the new winter house, so that was ready as well, one morning as I gave them their food.

George waved a piece of wood at me, and swiped at nothing in the air, I was not sure what he meant, but after a while of gestures, I finally got the message, "I think I'm thick at times" they had watched us playing bat and ball, with the grand children on the lawn, and wanted to do the same, they could copy anything, and after a little practice, do it quite well.

I went home to the playroom, and found a little dolly's bat and ball set, which seemed small enough, I showed them how to hit a ball to each other, they seemed to like the new game, so I left them to it, and when I told my wife, this amused her, "cheeky sods" she said, and we both laughed, "it'll be football next" she added, I also told her of my suspicions, "that they still go on hunting trips, not so much for food, but as a way of life" it has been three years, since the chicks first came to live with us, George my first contact with his kind, was I thought getting old, I'd often wondered what their lifespan was, it took a long time to find out, about seven years was average, poor old George was getting around slower these days, so I made him a pull along cart, they were happy to do this.

I also made George and his wife both bracelets, of dolly beads, because of the weight on their arms, Georges bracelet is of blue and white plastic pieces, his wife's of pink and white pieces, slid onto soft copper wire strands, what a job I had making them, it was a bit awkward at first to put them on, but they soon got the idea, and were glad.

To wear them, they were walking around, and I'm sure showing them off, they certainly got a lot of attention anyway.

I don't think that there was any jealousy with them, George was their leader and that was that, the bracelets also help me to identify them easier, and the one who is always with George, I made an all white bracelet.

His second on command I assumed, and the only difference I can make out between female and male, was the females were slightly smaller, and with a pot belly, as I call it, while the males were slim.

It has now been eight years, since the chicks first came, and things were going on alright at the present, there was only one bad incident for us, one morning, as I put the food and water down, I noticed them scuffling around, they were piling up leaves and twigs in a heap, then they laid George on it, puzzled, I connected up the radio system, "George, chick" I called, then the second in command came and spoke to me, "George gone to sun in sky" he said, and walked away, I was stunned and shocked, "George, gone" I repeated to myself, in disbelief, I went outside the cage and cried, I wept for my little furry pal, who with his race, had given us so much pleasure, I cried for a little while, then had to do some quick thinking, for their sake, and my own, "the second in command would have to be named George, like a bosses name, yes that's it" I thought, and went back into the cage.

I picked up George, very gently, and carried his little limp body down to the end of the area, scooped out some earth, and laid him in it, covered him over with earth, then laid some stones on top, the chicks were scampering about, probably wondering what I was doing, but watching me as I laid a primrose flower on the grave, and said a last goodbye to my friend George, I then put the radio near to George the second, and spoke to him, "next sun you be George" I said, "sss" he replied, as if knowing before me, I then left and went into the house, to make some more new bracelets, for the new George and his wife, when I told the wife the bad news, we both cried together.

It took a few more years to find out about the chicks, all their likes and dislikes, but all was well generally, and there are few problems now, as we live out our lives in a happy and contented co-existence, hopefully for my friends, the chicks,—forever.

GRANDMA

*I*t was a slightly breezy balmy day as I walked down the grassy lane to see my grandma.

At the door I was met by my cousin, I had not seen her for a few years, and never liked her anyway; I kissed grandma on the cheek and sat talking with a cup of tea made by Aimee.

We helped grandma outside to sit in her rocking chair on the veranda, it was nice in the shade looking over the garden and fields, we talked of the world for a while till grandma fell asleep, Aimee and I talked quietly, sitting close together so as not to waken grandma.

Aimee seemed a lot better now and not like the spoilt brat I last knew, we got on quite well, she told me that she was staying with grandma to look after her, well she was eighty eight, and said she knew our secret but would tell no one.

She knew now that I had been supporting grandma these last ten years financially, as her pension was rubbish and she would have starved without help, but would ask for none.

I had been putting money in her bank account each month, I earned a good wage so it didn't matter; I loved her and could not let it happen.

I had only found out by accident when I was here a long time ago, when grandma could not pay the gardener, I had paid him for the month, he always kept the gardens nice, grandma had cried and told me everything, it was then I vowed to help her and have done ever since, and will do so till she dies.

After I had finished telling Aimee she kissed me on the cheek, I was shocked and didn't move, "thank you from us all" she whispered and smiled, I think then I liked her more.

I lit a cigarette and sat thinking of the past, we all knew the bungalow was to go to Aimee, I used to resent it, but now it seemed right, wise old grandma had seen the good in Aimee, even as a spoilt brat, I didn't, but now understood why, as grandma had explained once, Aimee was as grandma was as a child, but now seemed as wise as grandma, it was uncanny and eerie, like grandma over again.

I knew they were both psychic, most of the family are including me at times, but grandma and Aimee seemed more so, they would just look at each other and know what the other one wanted, I had a good day with them both, and assured them I would visit as usual next weekend.

At work sitting at my desk, I pondered over them, the business ran itself mostly, so I had time on my hands, I made a few more contacts to supply computer parts to, and that was all I did all week, my manager sorts the orders out, and the secretary does the paperwork for packing, business was booming, the workforce of four people pack the orders, the courier van comes twice a week to take the boxes and that is it.

Sunday when I visited grandma and Aimee again, it was a cloudy day, so I drove up the lane this time in case of rain, Aimee greeted me with a kiss and I kissed grandma, Who always smelt of roses and not the age old lavender, which I was glad about, Aimee I noticed smelt of roses as well, we sat inside talking and laughing this day, I went home quite happy and glad Aimee was looking after grandma, who seemed much brighter now.

The following week went fine, with a large order from a supermarket, they had a super sale in a week's time, and we were all busy getting supplies in.

Packing and getting them ready for collection by one of their Lorries, I was glad when Sunday came again, for a rest we had all worked long hours including Saturday.

"A bonus" I thought "is what is needed as a thank you" I could easily afford it.

I was greeted as usual by Aimee and kissed grandma, we sat on the veranda today, grandma gave me some advice about not getting too big to soon, I made a mental note of it, and thanked her, and after all it was on grandma's advice that I started the business after talking to her about it.

I went home happy again and ready for next week.

I made sure they all had a good bonus, orders were starting to slacken off now, but we were still busy, getting things boxed up ready for the Christmas rush, and storing them on racks, this went on for a month, then we could relax again, I closed the place down for a weeks well earned rest.

No body seemed to mind, I spent the time with Aimee and grandma, I slept in the blue room as it's called, my fathers old bedroom.

It was quite a large bungalow, with four bedrooms, my father and aunties had been born and grew up there, I liked the place myself, and as a young lad my father had shown me the places he used to go to, his secret hiding place away from his sisters, favourite spots for swimming and fishing.

I had enjoyed doing the same things as he had done, on my summer holidays there, I know they all visit now and again with my other cousins, most younger than me, this I was glad about instead of forgetting about o.a.p's.

I knew grandma liked to see them all, she spoke of them on my visits, I spoke to Aimee about finances, not wishing to bother grandma, an increase was needed.

Now there were two of them, the council tax, electric, water and gas I always paid to save grandma worrying, grandma protested at first, but when I told her I could get tax relief on these things, she laughed but was thankful all the same.

After Christmas which I spent with my parents and sisters, I visited grandma again with my presents, Aimee spoke seriously to me while I smoked outside, "I think grandma will not have long to live" and her head dropped.

"I had thought the same myself" I admitted, "I shall have to sell the bungalow you know, I don't have a job to afford to live here, although I'd like to but" she stopped in mid sentence.

"Other people living in grandma's bungalow we can't have that can we, why not let things carry on as they are" I suggested, "I'll still pay like I do and keep up the allowance" she dried her eyes and kissed my cheek, "thank you" she whispered, I think it was all she could say.

She told grandma when we went inside, grandma had tears in her eyes, "I'm glad willum, you are doing this for us I was worried" "worry no more grandma" I kissed them both on the cheek, their smiles said enough, we sat talking over lunch, "why not come and live here willum.

You'll be company for each other, living alone is not always good"? grandma always called me willum, I think I'm her favourite grandson, I liked it, I said I would think about it and let them know, they smiled as if knowing the answer already.

I pondered the question while at my desk, writing down the pros and cons of everything, finally I decided to go and live there, after all I lived alone, I had bought my three bedroom house, assuming I would have a wife and family one day, but I had been too busy building up my business to think of women, and now at forty years old, the inclination didn't seem to be there anymore..

I spoke to them both about all this, "but you may want to wed one day surely willum"

"Maybe not grandma, I think I am too set in my ways now for anyone to consider me" "nonsense" was her reply, with a smile, "if I do move in here I may want to change some things" "that's fine by us" Aimee agreed with grandma, "I'll need a garage" "Fine" everything I suggested they agreed upon, I was getting my own way but I didn't like it very much.

I moved in two weeks later, put my house up for sale, it sold within a month, which was good for me, I was enjoying life and the company when not at work; I only go to the warehouse three days a week now.

All three of us had discussed an idea I had, we talked on it for several days, and I went to a solicitor and arranged for him to be at the warehouse on a Tuesday afternoon, at two o'clock, with all the staff to be there as well.

With my house sold I gave Aimee the cheque so she had money of her own, which she was grateful for, she would buy the food, and I would take care of the bills, a lot cheaper now with only one household to support, I had plenty of money to survive on, even if I never worked again.

It was good all round and worked out well, I was housed, had company and was better fed than when I lived on my own, grandma and Aimee were happy and so was I.

My new garage and workshop were built at the side of the bungalow, out of sight, and the lane is being laid with tarmac to make a proper road, especially for winter.

On the Tuesday in question I cleared my desk, laid out all the papers, ready to be signed and given to the staff, witnessed by the solicitor, after lunch when all were assembled, it was explained to them all, questions were answered, they signed and I signed all witnessed by the solicitor, we had a drink to celebrate the partnership deals, everyone was happy, my secretary cried, for joy I assumed.

"Now we are partners, you will be taught how to read a balance sheet, one evening a month is best I think, an auditor will be here to guide you through the process, and any changes you'll have to call a board meeting now and have it approved" they nodded in agreement and went home happy.

I was glad to be home my head ached, "all done Willum" "it is Aimes and I'm glad for it" Aimee calls me Willum now I don't mind and I call her Aimes, it was another year before grandma passed away, a very sad time for us two especially, a big empty space with nothing to fill it, business was going fine, so I took a holiday with Aimes to escape really, we saw places that each had always wanted to see, and learnt a lot about each other on the way.

When we arrived home after a month away, the bungalow was welcoming and seemed much brighter now, the cloud seemed to have lifted, or was it just us, I didn't care I was happy, it was the happy home I always knew when I visited grandma, like she was still here.

A year later at the warehouse I told them all "that I was going to fully retire, now they knew how to run the business" "you cant we need you" they protested, "no you don't, I've not done a thing this past year on purpose, you've all ran the business yourselves, if you think about it, all I will be is a honorary advisor if you need one" after much debate it was decided, a lump sum for my retirement, not that I needed it really, I tried to dissuade them, but was out voted and "had to accept the boards decision" as they were taught, so I did, they talked of employing more labour to take on bigger orders, I gave them the advice that grandma had given me, about getting too big too soon, it was up to them now.

I met one of them a few months later while out shopping, "no work" I asked, "plenty, we took you advice, have employed ten people now.

So we do not need to work anymore now, just live on the profits, we take it in turns to be there two days a week, that's all, and thank you for giving us the opportunity to do so".

I smiled and nodded, pleased with the way things were going.

I told Aimes when I arrived home, she was glad my time was not wasted.

We sat talking one evening, "its strange willum how things have worked out, especially for us, we live like brother and sister although we are not, but I am happy with life and you".

"I am Aimes, I think we were meant to be bachelor and spinster, grandma knew this I'm sure of it, I still miss her at times though" "me too bless her" we dried our eyes were always emotional when we talk of grandma, the wise old lady who knew and taught us so much, always giving and never taking.

I myself was glad and felt honoured to have known her and helped in her time of need, giving her a little back of the million things she gave us.

A much loved and missed lady, who no one could ever equal.

Invalids United

$\mathscr{I}$ had been talking with my fellow invalids, about our needs and independence, we had been talking for some time now, and as we all lived in the same six bedroom house, paid for by the government, it was cheaper for them this way.

two to a room, one in a wheel chair, one walk able, the rooms were big enough, and it worked well this way, we had a bedside cabinet and table lamp, a medium sized wardrobe, and a four tier chest of drawers each, a bed, a medium size table with two chairs, each room was equipped the same, courtesy of the government, I shared with Ian, who like me is a ten stone weakling, we call ourselves.

He's an electronics wizard, but because of his wheel chair, jobs are hard to find, some were dissatisfied with the way they were treated, but most accepted what they got.

Anything was better than nothing, we had been in touch with other groups of invalid's country wide, and one group had contacts abroad, which was good.

We had planned to travel to as many countries as possible, to set up contacts, with as many groups of people like us, as we could, but this would take a great deal of money, which we didn't have.

How to raise enough funds for the project, that was the next problem, we tried all the charities and government departments available, we got a little help, but not enough, by now we had exhausted all avenues of fund raising that we knew, how to get more money a problem.

We all had different skills, despite our disabilities, mine was organizing, I had been a transport organizer, for a big haulage firm, before becoming redundant, and at forty five, and disabled, I was considered unemployable, firms only wanted young go ahead managers these days, I was not necessarily the boss, but I could get things organized and done.

So I sent a letter to all the groups we knew, and they could pass it on to others, for any ideas of how to get extra funding.

It took several months for all the replies to get back to us, the first few, I laughed at, but most seemed to have the same answer, ROB A BANK.

I thought, "how could we invalids rob a bank, we cant run and escape in a car like able bodied people, bank robbers escaping in wheel chairs, ha, ha, a comic sight no doubt, we'd be caught within a few hundred yards".

But another thought occurred to me, "I wonder, is it possible, could we" I had a chat with the others, so purely as an exercise and amusement, I sent out letters to the groups, for ideas of how invalids could rob a bank, it would give us all something to do, and help pass the time, being disabled, at times can be boring and frustrating, sometimes the simplest task which ordinary people take for granted, can be a hard one for some of us.

Some of the ideas that came back were laughable, some ridiculous, but three, made me think, I contacted the three whose replies were feasible, and invited them to visit, at our groups expense, of course, after they had arrived I met them at the airport, and introduced myself, "hi I'm Bill" one was.

Alex, from Poland, Benny from Sweden, and Ranjit from India, when we arrived at the house, and they were settled in their room, we had changed the dining room around, they didn't mind a bit.

This was Ranjit and Alex's first visit to England, I took them to meet the rest of the gang, and introduced them, Ranjit had a false leg, Alex had a false arm, and Benny had two false legs.

There was Ian, in a wheel chair, brown straight hair, and our electronics expert, Neill, With a false arm, brown flat hair, stocky built, our master mechanic, Jasmine, a blonde, very artistic, despite her wheel chair, good at disguises.

Victor, good at accents, good at acting a roll, stocky built, but temperamental, and black curly hair, Dan, can get you anything within reason, slightly dappy, with his brown curly hair, was short and chubby.

David had a false arm, black straight hair, slim built, he was our master carpenter, Margaret, slim, brown curly hair, inclined to be depressive, but our main cook, Pat, chubby with blonde hair, but highly strung, Kim, was a bit chubby, brown haired, always ready for a laugh anytime, always cheerful, despite her wheel chair.

Shirley, with her brown neatly trimmed hair, in a wheel chair, can copy anything exactly, speaks French fluently, her mother was French, and a good forger if we need one.

Then Lily, bless her, a little chubby, and short, with black straight hair, our house keeper, always clearing up, dusting and polishing, then me, Bill, slim, one false leg, and the organizer, and planner, with brown curly hair.

We just chatted and had a drink, tomorrow we would take them on a sight seeing tour, of some places, the following day we had a meeting to discuss their ideas, and ways or means, because of the way some countries treat their disabled.

We wanted to help them, if we could, we didn't have a chairman or boss, we just bandied ideas around, to find a feasible solution, that all agreed to, or majority.

We came up with quite a few, but to put them in operation, that was the biggest problem, first we had to find safety deposit banks, check them all out, and see which were best.

Two of us sat across the road from five banks, as there were only ten of us available, we just sat around or stood talking, one in a wheel chair the other more able bodied.

and noting down open and close times, security guards, cameras, and anything else that might be useful, and buildings either side, we did this for a hour at a time, and listened to the security guards on their radios, after getting the wave length, with listening devices, and a special meter, all made by Ian our electronics expert, who takes notice of an invalid in a wheel chair anyway, they are nearly invisible to the public.

At the end of the week, we compared notes, to pick the best one, but we had two, these we checked out, both with a great possibility, which to go for? We voted, and came up both, "oh well" I announced, "in for a penny in for a pound" and our three visitors were happy to stay for as long as it takes, we were not just going for a little bank, but big ones, we were going for it, hook line and sinker.

Ian and Neill went to the first bank, they were shown down to the deposit room, and locked in, and had to ring the bell for the guard to let them out, as they were being led down to the deposit room, the hidden camera carried in the bag carried by Ian, was filming once inside the room, and the deposit locker opened, the guard left.

When on their own, Neill checked along the back wall with a sat nav, and an altimeter, so that we knew where the deposit room was, after putting these back in the bag, they called the guard and left the building, there was a basement flat next door.

A bit dingy but ok, Victor who is of Yugoslav decent, went to look over the flat, disguised by Jasmine.

While looking around, he took sat nav, and altimeter readings, he found that he was fairly level with the deposit room, so he rented the place, four hundred pounds a month; London prices sure were high, for a one bedroom flat.

When he got back to us, we checked the measurements, yep; he was right, and with the flat brick wall, a steel plate, then another brick wall, some task indeed, how to cut out bricks quietly.

Dan went and got engineering catalogues, where you can buy brand new or second hand equipment, we bought a small silent compressor, and an air operated hacksaw, with lots of different blades, David our carpenter, made a screen to cover the hole, not sure how he does it with one false arm, but he does and quite professional as well.

A box of latex gloves, these were to be worn all the time, it would take only one finger print, to foil the whole plan.

Ian and Neill went back to the bank, and down to the deposit vault, while me and Victor used the compressor and saw to cut away the mortar between the bricks, once in the vault Ian and Neill listened for any sound in the bank vault, at a pre-arranged time, me and Victor started to cut away the mortar, it worked quite well, they worked away for fifteen minutes, then stopped to await a phone call from Ian, who said "that nothing could be heard".

While the work was going on, Margaret and Pat were decorating the flat, with a little music, to disguise any sound from the compressor, should any one or other flat tenant visit, or look in the window, all would appear innocent, a new tenant, decorating the flat, and with the door shut between the bedroom and the living room, there was no sound of anything, while they worked away.

I went and purchased an old van, just about road legal, I got it from a second hand car dealer, for cash, and no questions asked, I also bought some sticky backed letters.

Lots of them, the plan was that some days it would be used as a decorators van, other days a plumbers van, it had three months road tax, and two months m.o.t.

Ian and Neill went to the second bank, rented a safety deposit box, and checked out the security, but this one had a security camera inside the vault, it only pointed at the door, which was lucky.

They put the envelopes in the box, took the sat nav and the altimeter readings, and after the usual questions that they asked the guard, they left the bank, next to the bank, was an office block, with two offices for rent, we chose the bottom office, on enquiring about the office.

A years lease, was the least option we could get, a bit expensive, a bit more than the flat, it was five hundred a month, we debated what to do, "yes or no" "yes" won, but only if it checked out ok, like the flat.

Victor and Neill checked out the office, and by the sat nav and altimeter readings, we would be just two feet below the vault ceiling, no good, unless we found a way, we discussed this and came up with an idea, "cut out the bricks, angling down wards, to make a bigger hole, this way we could do it, it would be difficult, but possible, the biggest problem was, how to open the safety deposit lockers, quickly and quietly as possible".

The security guards key would be the same for every locker, but each second key would be different, Acid seemed a solution, but that would take time to work, and time would not be plentiful, we had to be in and out as quickly as we could, air drills was the other option, although quiet, the drill bit would make a noise, not a lot, but maybe enough to be heard by the security guards, plenty of oil on the drills seemed to do the trick.

We lengthened the pipes on the air compressor, so that the compressor was not in the vault, but in the other room, and the air lines going through the wall into the vault, but we only had two air drills, we practiced at home drilling out locks, with diamond tipped drill bits, and got the time to fifteen seconds a lock, "not bad, not bad at all" I said.

But we had to get several drill bits, and by now our finances were getting low.

Ian and Neill went back to the first bank again, and down to the vault, while I cut through the steel plate, at a downward angle, with a gas torch, (oxygen and acetylene gas set,) which Ian had taught me to use, they watched for any discoloration on the wall, "none" was the answer, when they came out Neill stopped looked at some papers he was carrying, while the guard locked the door.

And with his back turned away from Ian, who planted a tiny listening device behind a metal table leg, this was to hear any noise that we would make during the robbery, or to hear a guard coming.

At the first bank, we had taken out the wall in the flat, cut a hole in the plate, and were ready to tackle the last wall into the deposit room, we had filled the hole with pillows, and covered it with a sheet of plaster board, to deaden any noise we might make, while waiting to do the job, it would take about three quarters of an hour to open the lockers, two on that job, and two to empty them, two to two and a half hours I had estimated for each job.

Including getting all the equipment out, and cleaning up, at the second bank, we had taken a years lease, on the premises, moved in some furniture, two desks with computer consuls, Shirley and Lily would pretend to be secretaries, but were really playing games on the computers, David our carpenter had made several screens, three to go round where we were taking down the wall, and two to make a screen between the door and the inner room, we took out the office wall, then some type of plaster. We came across a metal plate again, the other problem was.

Once we robbed one bank, all the banks would be checking their security systems, and maybe the police would check every building next to a bank, and this would not do, would it.

We would be discovered, and it would have all been a waste of time, rob both the same night, we had the time, but probably not the energy or drive.

A Saturday night would be the best time, more time to do the job, and not be found out till Monday morning.

At the office I had cut through the metal plate, quite easily really, it was only three eights of an inch thick, now both were ready, black spray paint for the camera lenses, lots of bottles of bleach for killing any scent, should the police use dogs, the guards rounds were ten, twelve, and three a.m. these were the times to stop work, we bought some builders polythene, which was thick, and made over shoes out of it.

These were to disguise any scent, and tread of our shoes, every thing was ready now, I checked over every detail, nothing missed that I could find, or had I missed something, one little detail, and all could be lost, this question puzzled me.

We practiced at home with mock ups, made of wood by David, getting in and out of the bank until we could do it quite well, next we went to the flat, to take away anything not needed, or we had used, cleaned the place thoroughly, and put fresh polythene down, then we did the same in the office, like a spring clean, took out the computers and desks, on the weekend chosen, Pat and Margaret went to different chemists, and bought calming drugs, the sort you can buy without a prescription.

But they also had their own prescription sedatives, for anyone to use, we were all getting a bit edgy, this waiting was nerve wracking.

We all had some tablets, washed down with a drop of scotch, it seemed to do the trick, everyone was calm when we set out, I set off with Victor, Neill, David, Ian, and Pat, we all knew exactly what to do, we had rehearsed our rolls several times at home, we didn't include our three visitors, partly because of language difficulties, also they had played their part in ideas, and helping with rehearsals.

I parked at the back of the flat, no back door, just a window, but it would serve our purpose, while Kim, Shirley, and Margaret, parked their van the other side of the bank, one would listen to the guards, on their wave band, one listening to the listening device, Ian had planted, and one to warn us when the guards did their rounds, Victor and Pat walked round the block to the flat, went in and opened the window, Neill passed in the folding wheel chair, then me and Neill carried Ian and passed him through the window as well, luckily for us it was a basement flat, and the window was only two feet from the ground, then we climbed in, closed the window and pulled the curtains.

"time for another pill" I thought, "right lads ten thirty, lets get to it" I said, Victor sawed out the remaining bricks into the room, I passed them to Neill who passed them to Ian, to stack them all neat and tidy, Ian checked if all was okay with the girls in the van, "yep ok" so we entered the security room, I crawled in first, unfolded the wheel chair and put the board down.

Victor came next pulling Ian along on a piece of polythene, which slid quite easily over the board, then we put him into the wheel chair, to do his bit, disconnect the door lock, so that even if we were discovered, they couldn't get in, and we could get away, hopefully, that was the idea.

And with my help we disconnected the smoke alarm.

Neill had started up the compressor; he put a blanket over it to deaden any sound, passed the air pipes and drills in then joined us.

While Pat sat in the other room, waiting for any messages from the others, and to pass them on to us, we were ready.

All nodded, it was decided before, that no speaking unless absolutely necessary, then only in a whisper, Victor and Neill began drilling out the locks, while me and Ian emptied the box contents, (not legal papers,) into pillow cases, these were stronger than bin liners, I checked my watch with my torch, we all had pen light torches, then went and checked with Pat "any news" I asked, she looked up from the magazine she was reading, "no news yet" then carried on reading, "huh" I thought, "that was a waste of time then" so I went and carried on emptying boxes, Ian and I were putting the pillow cases into bin liners, and stacking them at the hole, we seemed to be getting on quite well, I checked my watch again, eleven thirty, we should be finishing by now by my reckoning, I looked round the room, all the lockers were open, just the last twenty or so to empty, "another half hour should do".

"Clear up and be away by twelve thirty, not bad, not bad, wonder how the others are doing" all these thoughts went through my mind, I think that the adrenalines taking affect, more calm tablets were passed around, just in case, we got all the bags into the flat, me and Neill went back inside to wipe and spray every thing, while Victor loaded the van with the sacks, including the compressor and drills.

with Pat and Ian passing it all out the window, we had fifteen bags in all, having finished we handed Ian out the window, then all left as silently as possible, pulling the curtains and closing the window.

Both the vans exhausts had been wrapped in silencer bandages, and under the bonnet, so that very little noise was heard from the engines.

All the door locks and hinges had been well oiled for quietness as well; Pat spoke to Margaret, "to meet us at the office".

We arrived at the office, parked around the back, the other van did the same, "you girls okay" I enquired, "no were fed up and cold" was the nice sharp reply that I got, "never mind, here you can be inside and warm" I assured them, we got the folding wheel chair from the van, put Ian into it, wheeled him to the back entrance, dialed and opened the door, Ian and Neill went in first, closed the door, and Neill with Ian's help disconnected the door beeper, then opened up again for us all to go in, once we were all in the office, we had a stiff drink each, I checked my watch, and nodded, "now to work" Ian said wheeling himself over to the hole, I lit a cigarette that was needed as well, the smoke detectors had been disconnected when we first moved in, as before Victor cut away the remaining bricks, I handed them on to be stacked and covered, the girls helped out this time, making things quicker and easier.

At last we were through, it seemed a long time, but in reality it was only twenty minutes, Neill went in first, and laid down the board, then he went and sprayed the camera lens with the black paint, Victor followed next pulling Ian in, then me with the folding wheel chair, he put Ian in the chair, who went and disabled the door lock, and with Victors help disconnected the smoke alarm.

We were now almost ready to begin. Pat passed me down the air pipes and drills, I nodded then Victor and Neill began to open the lockers, me and Ian were emptying the boxes, when a voice whispered in my ear, "hello" this startled me and I almost dropped a box, as I jumped back in surprise, "sorry" Margaret said, "but me and Pat didn't want to miss all the fun.

We know what to do, we've watched you practice enough" "okay but" I gestured, "don't worry so much" she replied, "Kim, Shirley and Jasmine are listening out" I checked my watch, "one thirty, times getting on, must be away by three or soon after" I think to myself, "we've still got to drive home yet, that's about an hours drive".

We carried on working away, and the bags were being passed to Kim, who was sitting on the floor, then to Shirley, who stacked them by the office door.

But we were running out of pillow cases, so out I got, to go and empty some into cardboard boxes that the girls had in their van, I emptied ten, "should be enough" I queried to myself, I went back in and helped some more, checked my watch again, "two fifteen, three quarters of an hour left, before the security guard checks the premises" they only pull up in a security van, check the doors then go again, but we have to move the vans before then, further up the road, where they don't go, I got the keys from Margaret, and drove both vans up the road, out of sight.

"It's two forty five; after the guard has gone I'll drive them back".

At five to three we all sat down, and waited for the guard to come and go, he checked the front doors, then drove round to the back and checked the door, then left, "ok everyone, all clear" Jasmine whispered, we carried on, left the room, cleaned and sprayed every where, got the wheel chair ones in the vans first, and stacked the bags around them, wiped the wooden screens with dettol, to destroy any evidence, sprayed the office floor, wiped the door handle, and left the premises, feelings were running a little high now, adrenaline had taken over, we drove home, with all in high spirits, parked up, got everyone indoors.

Had a few stiff drinks, and a smoke, I was feeling a bit shaky as well, it took about an hour to wear off, the rest were calming down as well, I think "like me, most were knackered".

So we went to bed, and left Lily, Dan, and the others to clear up, I didn't wake till three p. m., only Dan, Lily and Jasmine were up.

Later in the day the rest got up, in the evening when we were all assembled, I made a short speech, "thank you all for what you have achieved these last few weeks, and especially this weekend" this was followed by lots of cheering and hand clapping, when this abated, I carried on, "I personally would like you all to talk about our adventure over the next few days, but for safety's sake, not mention it again, I think you will all agree with this, a wrong word in the wrong place, to the wrong person, and were all in trouble".

They all agreed, and were chatting away, I listened to some of the conversation's, and added bits of my own, it appears, that for all of us, including me, it was an exciting adventure, one we will never forget, all of us forgot our disabilities, and got on with the job in hand, Victor showed no temperament at all, he enjoyed it, Margaret, often depressed, was not depressed at all, in fact quite happy, Pat who can be hysterical, seemed happy and quite calm, the rest of us were okay, but still a little excited, just talking about it, so I concluded "that the excitement and adrenaline rush during the robbery, was what we all needed".

On Monday, we all watched the news, especially about the two bank robberies; the police could find no clues anywhere.

Only they were looking for a foreign man by the name of Dubchik, "good old Victor " Pat said, amid a few more cheers, "we've done it, the perfect robbery" Kim added, voicing our thoughts, "yes" I conjectured, "but Shirley, David and Neill still have to go to France and Switzerland, before we can use the money, some we'll keep for expenses, but the rest must go, and the jewellery has to be broken up, and disposed of".

This was followed by a lot of grumbling, "I have thought of a way out of the problem, but I will need the assistance of you all" this perked them up a bit, and they were all eager for my solution, and more adventure, I continued, "Shirley, David and Neill, to go to France, and Switzerland, Shirley can visit her friend Francis maybe stay a few day's, would you like that" I enquired, "oh yes please" she smiled, "I'll give her a ring and arrange it" I carried on, "right now David and Neill will have to do a bit of sight seeing, and meet us at the cliffs just from Boulogne sur mer.

Where we will hand over the suit cases of money, I'll arrange a boat for two days, like when we have our outings, probably the same one, but here's the tricky bit, we have to rendezvous at night, in total darkness, and get the money ashore, up the cliffs really, like smugglers, without being caught.

We'll have to go from Rye harbour, follow the coast round to Folkestone, then across to France, I'll show you all, on the maps, the waters quite deep there, and we can get within two hundred yards, someone will have to row out in the dinghy, and tie the suit cases to ropes, for David and Neill, to pull them up, although I've said David and Neill, I chose them because there's a lot of driving to do, but if anyone wants to swap around, it's no problem, I'll leave you all to talk it over, I still have some arrangements to make".

left the room, and went outside, for a smoke and a think, "tomorrow night we'll take the vans to a derelict factory site, due to be demolished, for a housing estate, and we'll burn them out, the police will think it's just yobbos as usual, take a car for a joyride then set light to it".

Over the next few days we discussed how much to give Ranjit, Alex and Benny, so we asked them what they most wanted in life, Ranjit, wanted to buy a ten bedroom house he knew of, for family and disabled friends.

Alex, a new tractor and ploughs, for the farm, and a house extension.

Benny, two new rooms added, and a new kitchen, also a holiday for his family.

After much discussion, it was decided that a hundred thousand would suffice.

They were over whelmed when we told them, Alex would accept a bank transfer, Benny would accept a cheque, But Ranjit, banking was not his thing, and carrying a suit case full of money, was out, a little more difficult, so he accepted jewellery instead, which he could sell, to raise the necessary cash, all this would be stuffed into his hollow false leg, I think we gave him more than enough, he kept saying "thank you, thank you" which got a bit boring after a few days.

About two weeks later, when all was arranged and settled, we hired a decent car for the trip abroad, and put five thousand into Shirley's French bank account, which we always use on holidays, this would give them more than enough for the journey, and hotel expenses, although they will be away up to a month, on the day of departure, after they had boarded a ferry to France.

We hired a mini bus and driver to take the rest of us to Rye harbour and the boat, at the boat I paid Stephen the owner five hundred pounds for the hire, as fishing was limited, he didn't mind a little extra cash. we had hired his boat before, and he trusted us with it, it was a good fishing boat, with a boom for unloading the catch, but we used it to winch the wheel chair bound aboard, we were finally set, all nine of us, Lily, Dan and Ranjit had stayed at home, they didn't like the sea, off we went, nice and steady as always, once on the open sea Victor had a go at steering, following the coast line, Jasmine and Ian acted as lookouts for other boats, we always gave way to them it's safer.

We all had a change round about every two hours, stops the boredom, we have to take all day before we reach the rendezvous point, on the French coast, we can't get there before night fall, it would be to early, we reached the spot at dusk, pulled into the cove, dropped anchor and waited.

Neill phoned, they were at the top of the cliffs, Victor and me, we were to go in the dinghy with the cases, the others kept watch for any other boat approaching, or a customs launch, we rowed to the cliffs in the bay, I gave one flash with my torch, and two flashes came from the cliff top, down came a rope, I tied it around the first suit case, gave a tug on the rope, and it went up and disappeared from view.

It came down again for the second case, then the third, then three flashes from above and one from me, we left and rowed back to the boat.

After we had stowed the dinghy away, "boat coming" Pat said, we just sat down in the cabin with a drink, Kim kept an eye on the other boat, "gone right past" she announced, so we celebrated that night, drinks all round, someone started singing "what shall we do with a drunken sailor" we all joined in, spirits on a high, we were singing when a voice from the door way said, "eenglish" turning we saw a French customs officer, we just started to laugh, someone said "oui" he just waved his arms French style, said "eenglish" again, and left, we carried on celebrating, nine of us in a little cabin, some on the bunk beds, one or two standing.

Some sitting on chairs at a small table, a bit cramped, but we enjoyed it, although we must have looked strange to the customs officer.

I woke at ten a.m. went up on deck, washed my face in cold water, Kim and Pat were already there, "how did you get up the stairs" I enquired, "on my bottom backwards" she laughed, when the rest were all up, some of us a bit stiff, having slept on the floor. I started the engine, and headed back to England, Margaret phoned the mini bus company and arranged to meet us at Rye harbour at seven p.m. to take us back home. Three weeks later David rang, they were on their way back, having deposited the money in a Swiss bank, and sold the bearer bonds on the open market, when they arrived home, we began to sort things out, and to help those that we originally intended to, with seven million at our disposal, we could help a lot, it should go quite far.

We all put our share together and bought a old farm house, quite cheap, which needed renovating, most liked the country, it had outbuildings, and here we would each have our own room, some their own little cottage, yet to be sorted out who, it will take us quite a while to finish, but worth it in the end, a new mini bus from motability, converted to take wheel chairs.

As the house was in Shirley's name, we rented the place from her, as far as the authorities were concerned.

We put our rent allowances together, this paid the poll tax, gas and electric bills, I think we are a scheming lot sometimes, but then you have to be these days, to get anywhere, or anything.

But in reality Shirley had written and signed a disclaimer, because she had wanted to, so that to sell the farm in the future, all would have to agree.

We had just finished the farm house, and were getting ready to move in, we had a letter from Ranjit; he had bought the house, had two poor families and some friends living there, and fed them all, he was looking to buy some more houses; we certainly over paid him, no matter though.

Alex, had his new tractor, according to his letter, and was having a new house built, instead of an extra room.

Benny, well, we will be seeing him later in the year, were taking a holiday in Sweden, maybe look at some banks on the way, ... Who knows?

LITTLE ANIMALS

As we stood looking at the house, I wondered what jobs there were to do.

we looked around inside, it needed a lot of modernising and painting, I checked every room making notes as I went, one room was cluttered, furniture with odds and ends everywhere, I heard a scuffling sound "ha mouse traps needed as well" I thought made a note and left the room.

It took a few weeks of hard work and a lot of expense before I finally got to the cluttered room again, I had left it till last on purpose, I started by taking out old furniture and burning it, "that's our home you're destroying" a voice said behind me, "I'm sorry I didn't know" I replied and turned around, the room was empty, "is this place haunted" I thought, "no its not" the voice answered "what" I replied looking for someone hiding somewhere, could find no one.

"We are here near you" I sat down on the floor, something touched my leg, looking I saw a toy dinosaur, but it moved, "they'll need new batteries soon" I muttered to myself, "we do not need batteries, were real idiot, the professor said to be careful of humans just before he died" explained the voice, I sat stunned not believing what I was hearing, "I'm going bonkers" I told myself, "no you're not just accept us as we are" was the reply, looking round I saw several coming from their hiding places, "what the bloody hell" I said, my mind confused, I think then I panicked and left the room.

Went for a stiff drink and a smoke, it took a while for me to calm down and collect my thoughts, "was that real or me just being stupid" I thought, but curiosity got the better of me in the end, I had to find out for certain.

It was two days later before I ventured into the room again, fully prepared for anything, voices, little dinosaurs or anything else there might be.

I had made sure that I was the only one working there that day, just in case of anything nasty happening.

I opened the door cautiously, walked in the room and sat on the floor, "hello again" the voice said, "better now" "I am after the initial shock" I replied, "we are speaking to you telepathically, like we were taught and were starving were all vegetarians and require food, then we will tell you all" "right" I muttered and left the room to find them something to eat.

I found some vegetables in the garden dug them up took them back with some grass as well, and a few dandelions, put them on the floor and sat again, I counted eight of them, all eating lots "lovely" a voice said, "but we eat leaves as well".

I went and cut a few branches off of some trees that were around the place, I took an arm full and a cabbage that I found, put them down and sat to wait.

It took a little while for them to finish eating, I had a smoke while I waited it didn't seem to bother them at all.

Once they had finished, they came and sat down beside me, one of them told me their story, the professor, who they called father, had created them from the d.n.a. taken from fossil bones and dinosaur eggs found all over the world, he had been with a team of researchers, checking all the finds for a university, they told me his name, but I didn't know it, I could research it on the internet later, he had made them small on purpose, after a lot of trial and error, kept them here in secret of course, I said that I must go but would be back in a few days with more food, rose and left the room.

Had another smoke and a drink, sat and pondered over what had happened and I was told telepathically.

I was okay psychologically, but still a bit apprehensive as to what to do about them, or what they really wanted.

I arrived three days later with lots of vegetables, pulled leaves off of trees, went to the

Room put it all down and sat, they appeared and ate away, "lovely" they said, they told me a little more of things and how they had been hiding from people, finding food where ever they could.

Heard us come in and had altogether pushed the door shut, till I arrived, they had been as surprised as I was at our first meeting, "we would like to be outside, we've tried it once but its far too dangerous for us" "I'll see what I can do, I'll have a look around to find a safe place if you like" "yes we would".

I went outside carrying one of them, "this is where we've been before" it was a small fenced off area, "I could put small squared weld mesh all around the area to make it safe if you wanted" "what is this weld mesh" "I will bring some here then you can see my friend" "my names Ogee" "and mines Nick" "well Nick it would be nice if it works" "I'll be back in a couple of days, you'll need more food by then" "we will and thank you from us all".

I took Ogee back to the room, locked the door and went home.

I returned two days later with lots of weld mesh and poles ready for the enclosure, laid the weld mesh out for the dinosaurs to see, took a box with me to the room, put them in and took them outside to see the weld mesh, "that would be nice Nick, we'd be safe inside that" "I thought you might" and smiled, "keep out of the way please as I cannot see you in the long grass, and don't wander far" "we'll not Nick" I started to knock the poles into the ground at set paces, it took two whole days to complete the area, and a few more days to fix the weld mesh on, more poles I put in to support the roof, put a small dish in for water, at last after more than a week it was finished.

I took them to the enclosure put them into it, they disappeared in the long grass; I tipped the vegetables in and locked the door.

Leaving them to do what they wanted, I left them alone for a while just putting vegetables in every two or three days, after a few months when the house was finished and we all moved in, I told the family "that the weld mesh area was for little animals to be safe in" this they accepted and left it at that, for me it was much much more but they never knew the real secret.

MY CURSED DAY

As I looked out the window, thoroughly fed up with nothing to do, "clean out the garden shed" I thought.

It was a bit cluttered and I moaned to myself every time I went in there, so resolutely and with good intentions I opened the shed door, the rake handle hit me on the head, I cursed pulled it out with a few more tools and laid them on the lawn, pulled out the mower with a jerk and banged my shins, another curse followed it.

I took a few more things out laid them out side on the lawn, stood on the rake end and another bang on the head, with a curse.

Picked up a paint pot which was stuck to the floor that spilt over my foot as I yanked it up and the handle came off in my hands, another curse from me.

Picked up a box of nails, which split and nails went over the floor, picking them up I stuck my hand on one, another curse came, that done I put the box outside.

Swept the floor, it was looking good now, as I started to clear the shelves I pulled another paint pot which was stuck and the shelf came down with it, spilling paint, varnish and odds and ends every where, as I lay on the floor in a sticky mess, I cursed several times.

Got up and went indoors for a bath, the wife laughed at me, "you went out all nice and clean and return covered in paint, limping and a bandaged hand" more laughter from her, "it's a war zone dear, better get someone to do it for you" I grumbled and went for my bath carrying a black rubbish bag to put my clothes and shoes in, "I'm having a cursed day" I told myself.

As I climbed into the bath my foot slipped on the bottom and I did the splits, banging the dangly bits on the side of the bath, more cursing.

Watery eyed, at last I lay in the bath, the soap slipped out of my hands and landed on the floor, I leant over to retrieve it, and ended up my head on the floor, feet still in the bath and the dangly bits of me squashed on the top of the bath again, ... it took at least ten minutes to get back in the bath with a sigh of relief as the pain eased to allow me to wash.

I got out the bath and stood on the soap where I had left it, fell out the bath with more cursing.

Later that day two lads came to do the job, it took them a few hours, on inspection it was clean, garden tools hanging up, "very nice lads thank you" I paid them for the work, they went away quite pleased.

I shut the shed door and caught my shirt cuff on the handle, yanking my arm, I pulled my arm away and ripped the shirt sleeve, after I had finished cursing, I vowed never to go near the shed again, but get someone to do the gardening for me.

"I'll put up with the boredom" I thought, as I walked indoors with my shirt sleeve in tatters, more laughter from the wife, went to change my shirt tripped up the stairs banging my shin, a silent curse followed put my hand on the hand rail to pull myself up, my hand slipped and I banged my elbow, another silent curse.

Heard more laughter from the wife, As I took a shirt from the hanger, three others fell on the floor, I bent to pick them up and banged my head on the wardrobe door, cursed, slammed the door shut, it fell off its hinges and hit me in the face, more cursing, as I got up.

tripped down the last three steps as I went down stairs, landed on my rump, which hurt, the wife just smiled as she handed me a cup of coffee.

The handle came off and I was soaked and burnt in the nether regions, I silently cursed a few times, some one laughed again.

I went to change, being doubly careful of every thing, I changed and went to the back door to have a smoke, stubbed my toe on the step, cursed, lit a cigarette and singed my eyebrows, and more curses followed that.

Sat in my chair careful of the cup, amid laughter at my singed eyebrows, "I'll be glad when today's over" I thought, turned the telly on, the screen was fuzzy, so I thumped it on the top, it went off and smoke came from the back, I unplugged it and that was that, no sport to watch today.

"We need a new one anyway dear" the wife spoke and laughed, I grumbled and sat on the cat, which had jumped onto my chair, I jumped up, banged my knee on the coffee table, cursed silently as the wife laughed.

"Not your day dear"she laughed again," it's definitely not, it's my cursed day had I replied.

As I went to bed I put my pyjama jacket on inside out, silently cursed as someone giggled while reading her book.

I read the pages that I wanted to, went to turn out the bed side light, knocked it on the floor, another silent curse followed, I was glad to go to sleep, ending my cursed day.

A builder arrived the next day to fix all the little jobs that I never got around to doing, including the wardrobe door, a new telly was installed by the weekend, and things were fine, no more breakages, bumped heads, torn shirts or paint spillages, it was heaven.

MY DAY

~~~~~~~~~~~~~~~~~~~~~~~~~~~~ ◦◦◦◦ ~~~~~~~~~~~~~~~~~~~~~~~~~~~~

*A*fter working for myself for a number of years, I had built up a small business, doing property maintenance, building and electrical work.

And now employed two men, on a permanent basis, they weren't the best but had to do.

If I needed any more help, then I knew some more self employed men like me, who would always help out, for a price, of course, and the same applied visa versa.

I had got a contract for about a month, in my estimation, to empty a large warehouse,

Which had stood empty for a few years?

When we opened the main doors, it was stacked full of broken furniture of all sorts, we would have to start at the doorway and clear a way into the building, smashing it all up and putting it into skips to be taken away, I would have burnt it but environment regulations in the area prevented it.

We started on a Monday morning, by unlocking the steel doors and forcing them wide open, a whole lot of oil is needed on them, "were not having this task every morning" I thought to myself, which was one of the jobs I did while the other two cleared away some rubbish, the two skips arrived and were dropped alongside the building, ready to be filled, we began, talk about dust, dirt and spiders, what a mess.

We had to break up the old wooden chairs that were stacked in each other, a bit like a Chinese puzzle, as if done deliberately, I wondered "what bloody idiot did this, and why"?.

As we started clearing out the warehouse I left the other two to it, while I oiled the hinges and got the doors working reasonably well, having got that done we had a tea break and a cigarette.

Afterwards the work was a bit mundane, for the rest of the day.

And now with two skips full of broken wood and nothing more to do, we went home.

On Tuesday morning, having waited for the skips to be changed, we started in again, by about midday enough room was cleared inside to make working comfortable, instead of standing on each others toes, John pointed, "look through there" we looked and saw large sheets of polythene hanging from ceiling to floor "maybe some decent furniture behind that" he said.

We carried on smashing but making a bee line for what would be the center of the room, by about five p. m. we reached it, slitting open the polythene and looking inside, then we swore as working men do.

"No furniture here, just metal plates" John checked then I checked, I lifted one, "it's aluminium we'll get a few bob from the scrap yard for this, you can bring the truck tomorrow" "right was the reply" so we finished for the day, locked up and went home.

Wednesday morning came, a dull looking day, probably rain but luckily for us Monday and Tuesday were fine so off to the warehouse we went.

Changed one skip for the other, the empty skip we pushed inside the building with the truck, parked the trucks rear end just inside the doors, I carried on smashing and loading the broken furniture, while the other two John and Dave loaded the truck with plates, after loading the truck quite full, they then took the load to a scrap merchant we knew, about ten miles away.

But now we were inside, there was not as much furniture as I first thought, by the time they arrived back, about three hours later the skip was quite full.

The truck pulled up, and Dave got out of the cab grinning like a Cheshire cat, but John staggered out and fell in a heap on the floor, like a discarded rag, I knew he liked a drink, but not that much in the day time, "bloody drunken idiots what's up with you two" Dave just stood there grinning.

"Your just a couple of pissheads" and remembered that I had a couple of occasions in the past with them like this.

"Sorry mate, but we got a few extra bob each and wanted to celebrate" John muttered, "just sit there you two and sober up" I grumbled, "if this is how it's going to be every time they take a load, no way" I thought, "if this happens again, your both sacked, and where's my share of the scrap money" "we spent it" was the slurred reply, "stupid idiots" I thought, and went to work, putting a rope around the skip and towing it outside ready for the morning, afterwards I backed the truck inside, "they aren't driving that home tonight" I locked up and drove them home.

Thursday morning came a fair day weather wise, but I was dubious after yesterday's performance by the two twits, I knew time would tell and resolved to get on with some work, we finished loading the truck and they went off to the scrap yard, while I broke up more furniture.

They were back in about two hours, we loaded up the truck with the last load, and they went out again.

I climbed up my stepladder which we brought with us and began cutting down the polythene to clear it out of the way, it was hard work but at last it was done, I threw it into the skip "another load for tomorrow" I muttered to myself, by now time was getting on I looked at my watch five o'clock already, where's that bloody truck got to.

More muttering to myself, "sod it" I thought, "I'm going home" I got home and there was the truck, standing in the yard, keys in the ignition, but no sign of anyone.

"They're both sacked" I said aloud and did some more muttering to myself, I was livid, if anyone had heard me they'd think I was loony talking to myself.

Friday came and I had a message on my mobile phone, it was from Dave and John they had quit and with the few hundred they got from the scrap yard were going on a binge, "good" I said aloud "and don't expect any wages and don't come back either" I went to the warehouse and cleared away the remaining furniture in this part of the place, pulled the skip outside with the truck, drove the truck inside and parked up, lifted down the generator with a struggle, and rigged up some lights, started up the generator which was of the silent type, and flicked the switch to light up the place. Looking down a corridor to my right, I could see a door at the end, and another half way down in the wall and not having any keys.

I attacked the far door with a crowbar, it gave way I looked in, not much in here, just an old desk and chair, probably the office, I pulled it out with lots of dust and threw it in the skip, it was about two o'clock by now and I had decided to have an early day for a change.

Made a note of what was needed for Monday, industrial Hoovers, brooms, and rubbish sacks, this should do to clear up the place, and I would see a couple of mates as well, time was getting short, and on my own I would not make the deadline.

On Monday morning having hired two industrial cleaners, I went back to the warehouse, and started to clean up the small office at the end of the passage, I had just finished it when my mates arrived, "good, brush the ceiling and walls down first then we'll Hoover the floor" while they were cleaning the place, I tried to open the other door, trying the crowbar, no good next trying an axe, it splintered the wood a bit, so I got out the chainsaw.

This bit into the wood about an inch, then sparks flew in the air with a grinding noise, I soon stopped, "oops" I muttered to myself, then I cut out a piece of wood, prized it out with the crowbar, and looked, a bloody steel door, "sod it that'll take some opening" I muttered aloud, I next tried the door frame, the same thing steel, I tried the wall, which was of the soft internal block, I first hacked out a sizeable chunk with a hammer and chisel guess what, bloody metal plate again.

"Right I told myself, tomorrow I'll bring cutting gear" so I left the door for the day and went to help the others brushing down, we got the ceiling brushed down, then went home, dusty and dirty, but happy.

Next day armed with a small cutting torch, I had resolved to open that door, one of the others turned the door handle as he walked past, and pushed the door open about two inches, then it got stuck, "there" he said, "try it yourself mate" after much Mickey taking, because I hadn't even tried the door handle, but it was stuck fast.

"ha, the gas set wont be a waste of time after all, I'll warm up the hinges and oil them while hot, then It'll open" I replied.

Justifying myself, as I was doing this a shout came from the direction of the main doors.

"Morning, you're getting on well I see" I turned and saw it was Mr Goodsal, the man who had given me the contract to clear the place, as I walked over to the door, I called the others to follow, "tea time" I called, that's all it takes, two magic words.

I met Mr. Goodsal at the door, and offered to show him around, but he declined the offer, don't blame him with his nice suit on, but asked "what's inside?".

"There's a room at the end of the corridor, which I had to break into," I apologized for that, "no problem" he replied, "throw it in the skip" "and another half way down which I'm trying to open, should be cleaned and empty in about a week or so" hoping to finish as soon as possible, "good, I'll send your cheque by the weekend" "lovely" I thought "nice bit of profit, keep me going a few months".

Then he offered us liquid lunch at the local pub, we went, glad to be away from the dust for a while, lunch went down well, we thanked him and went back to work.

Slightly happier and jovial, the blokes went back to brushing down the walls, and I went back to the door, pushing it enough to get in, then I set up a light from the generator, warmed up the hinges some more, and forcing the door open then working the door open and shut until it worked quite easy, stepped into the room with the light, looking around, "hmm, not much here either, just cobwebs and lots of dust, over the desk and floor like the other bloody room" I grumbled.

The desk was in a corner, it was covered in what looked like lumps of dust boxes and bags covered in dust on the floor, it was about four thirty, "lets call it a day lads" I shouted, so we did.

Wednesday morning was much the same weather wise, dull and cloudy, glad I'm working inside I muttered to myself, first job, taking the broken door and binning it, in the skip, I got out the small Hoover that I had brought for the purpose of cleaning the room.

I started to clean at the end of the first, and working my way past the desk to the middle, that's better, now over some of the boxes and bags that littered the floor.

Clunk, and the Hoover screeched, turning off the Hoover, I separated the tubes, and found a large brooch and chain, stuck in the first bend, hmm, it looks genuine, I thought, stuffing it in my pocket, finders keepers, was the motto.

I reassembled the Hoover and opened a lid on one of the old ammo boxes, and shut the lid quickly, "bloody hell" I said aloud, the mind racing at a fast pace.

If what I've just seen is right, I'm rich; I went and had a cupper and cigarette, just to steady my nerves.

The lads joined me, "soon have this place finished" they said, "good, don't worry, I'll pay you at the weekend anyway" after our lunch break I checked out the room, the lumps of dust were pieces of jewellery, just lying around on the desk, I put a few pieces in my pocket and put the rest into a sack, then checked the boxes on the floor, all were full of I think gold bars, ingots is the word, but I wasn't taking any chances, false or not.

I switched off the light and shut the door, the lads would be today and tomorrow, then I could check things out in this Aladdin's cave, which the old bloke had before he left, apparently he had been a scrap dealer, who was frequently in London, before suddenly dropping down dead with a heart attack, this is according to Mr. Goodsal, when we went to the pub the other day with him.

Scrap dealer, more like a fence, as their called in the criminal world.

By Thursday morning the lads had finished the walls, so I gave them a hand to finish the floor, then home.

"See you Friday night for some dosh" "okay and thanks lads, nice job" "good" I thought "with them gone, I could carryon with making the place secure, Wasn't taking any chances, especially now" I locked up with a large padlock that I used when the truck was left inside, then went home, on the way home I went to a secure industrial site I knew.

On reaching home I parked the truck, and got out the land rover, "this would be better for moving the goods, and as I would be out of the premises soon" I thought "it's covered and away from prying eyes".

In the morning I went to a local jewellers, and asked if he could "do an appraisal for insurance purposes" and that I would be back tomorrow morning, then drove to the warehouse, unlocked, drove the land rover inside and started up the generator for lighting, closed and barred the main doors with some four by two timber I had brought for the purpose, having done this, "right" I thought, "lets go to it" now I could work undisturbed, I got the sack barrow and plank from the rover, set up the plank as a ramp into the back of the rover then wheeled the sack barrow into the room, now to start work, as I slid the first box onto the barrow, phew, must weigh a hundredweight, I thought, then wheeled it out to the rover, slid it up the ramp and into the back, I did this ten times, had a break, this was hard work for one, I also loaded three sacks of bits of jewellery and the pieces of jewellery that I found lying around, then I locked up the rover, finished hoovering the room, put it in the rover, this took up more time than I thought.

I drove outside locked the doors and drove to the secure site, where I had asked for a secure workshop yesterday, I paid a years rental in advance, this speeded up the paperwork, I went to the security office, picked up the keys drove round to the unit, opened up the door then the roller shutters and drove in.

Closed the shutters and padlocked them, went and locked the door then parked over by the far wall beside a sink unit, then I went out set the alarm, went to meet the lads at a pub paid them and bought a drink.

Saturday I went to the jewellers in town, I arrived as arranged just on lunchtime.

As I walked in the jeweler looked up, "ah, I wont keep you a moment" he walking round the counter locked up the shop, then said "follow me" he led the way into the back of the shop and into his workshop, "have a seat" he motioned me to a chair at the bench, which I did.

He sat down facing me across the bench, "this bunch of jewellery that you have brought me is worth about two hundred and fifty thousand pounds, the large brooch encrusted with diamonds and set in gold and platinum, I thought that I recognized it, from a police circular a few years ago, I should inform the police, but I would like to know a little more how you came to have it, before I decide what to do".

After I got over the shock at the price he had given me, and what he had just said, I told him "that I had found it hidden in a wall, with other jewellery in a house that I had bought, and I was renovating it to resell at a profit".

"The owner had died and his family wanted to sell it to get some money, I had bought it cheap for a quick sell, so they couldn't have known about the jewels, could they" he nodded, "there's more than what I've shown you, that's why I came to find out what they're worth" "hmm" he muttered, I could see what was going on in his mind, money, otherwise, a mister plod would have been waiting for me at the door, I sort of guessed what was coming next, "to avoid detection, this brooch and other pieces like it would have to be split up and the gold and platinum melted down, which is about half the price" "okay" I replied.

"Do you know anyone who would do it for a fifty fifty split" putting the question to him, although I had guessed his reply, "yes" he muttered, eyeing me warily, "don't worry mate, nobody knows about it, and nobody wants to go to jail do we".

I ventured, "No" he muttered again, slightly embarrassed, "good, cos there's a whole lot more and some, where that came from"

He looked at me, raised his eyebrows, and said, "we all need money, and now we understand each other, lets get down to business" I said "and that I would show him a sack full of the stuff, later or on Monday, if he cared to let me take him there".

To the secure unit was the best bet, I picked him up outside his shop as arranged later that day, went to the secure site, checked with security to turn off the silent alarm, went to the unit, drove in and closed the shutters.

"This is where I have been storing and cleaning it all, it's quite safe here" he looked at the jewellery and stones that I had cleaned up, then at the other sacks of stuff that I had, "phew" he whistled, through his teeth, "must be a million or two's worth here" I had guessed as much already, "and there's more, must have been a busy crook".

"Bloody hell" he gasped, "I'll have to be careful disposing of this lot" then I showed him a gold bar, "what's this worth then" I asked, he looked at it, tested it, "unmarked, hmm, worth about seventy five thousand off hand I'd say" "good, co's I've got eighty bars of the stuff" "what" he shouted, "oh Christ" and sat down heavily on the rover tailboard.

After a little while in thought, he said "we'll have to be doubly careful" his panic leaving him, but still a little pale, after smoking a cigarette.

"let's talk, jeweler's buy and sell gold, silver and stones to each other all the time, yes that's what we'll do, and we all know shady dealers as well, should be about a few million split, but will take about a year to do, to be safe, I will open a separate account so you can see there's no fiddling on my part" "fine by me".

"Then he added that his wife had wanted him to sell up and close the shop, that he inherited from his father anyway, this would be a good time to do it, as the trade wasn't very good, and his friends, and they wouldn't be surprised at his sudden wealth".

As for me, I would pick the right week to tell friends that I had won a few million on the lottery, when there were one or two winners, that would be just about right, next week I would hand the keys to Mr. Goodsal, my last job of work for anyone, and after a year, suddenly become wealthy, and then it would really be, MY DAY.

MY GENTLE LOVE

I think it all started a few months after starting a new job.

At first she was just another member of staff, she was not a beauty that men would wolf whistle at, just ordinary, brown haired, about five feet six tall, medium build.

I used to play jokes and wind up everyone, until recently, then she would blush if I came near or looked at her, I liked it but didn't know why?.

I used to get a tingling feeling inside, a bit like butter flies or nerves in the stomach, and it gradually and slowly grew and grew, until after about a year, I knew that I loved her, mind, body and soul, sometimes it became an all consuming passion.

I couldn't concentrate on my work, I even started to be bad tempered and moody, so I had to check myself, which was very difficult, but I managed it, after all it wasn't her fault, it was me, just being a stupid old man, to think that a young woman could ever think of me other than a work colleague.

I resolved to admire her from afar, after all she was a single woman making a career for herself, and I was a married man, ten years older, in a rocky marriage.

I should have known better, but there was something about her that disturbed me.

at one time it appeared that we hated each other, it soon passed.

It was probably frustration of sorts, on my part of course, but I knew that I had to speak to her about how I felt, if she slapped my face and called me a dirty old man, then I would have left the job, but keeping it to myself was driving me nuts, and causing me all sorts of physical and mental pain, but I really hoped that she would not be too offended, and that we could at least be friends, this would be the best I could expect, at least I'd see her every day.

I was repairing some fluorescent light fittings in the main store room, which some idiot had smashed with the fork lift, while playing around; he was sacked on the spot of course.

It was a bit dim where I was working, I had a lead light as there were fifteen light fittings working, the other twenty were either smashed or wires pulled out, the store was large, it could take delivery of about eight lorry loads of goods, the stock had been removed from this part to allow me to do repairs, I was to work late, to get as much done as possible before the night lorry loads came in.

I was working away, sometimes whistling to myself or singing, trying to get more of the store room lit, she had walked in, unnoticed by me, checking the stock was her job, as stock controller.

I was rehearsing that which I wanted to say to her, I had rehearsed it maybe twice, I don't know, I thought that I was alone, and was speaking out loud, I looked at my watch, and thought "tea time" then as I turned round to go to the canteen, there she was just standing there.

The tears in her eyes, were just starting to trickle down her Cheeks, and the most gentlest smile that I have ever seen on a woman's face.

Much like that of a child who trusts you with their life, they look up into your eyes with that gentle loving, innocent smile, that can melt ice.

I know that then I blushed, and wished the floor would open up and swallow me, I tried to apologize, but I just stuttered,

"I'm, I'm sorry, I, Ium, I didn't want you to know er to, to bloody hell" I swore, "I've tried not to, but I love you" my senses were muddled, enough by now, and I felt ashamed, not daring to say anymore, I've already made a hash of things, then I gently touched her cheek to wipe away a tear, I moved back from her and turned to walk away, to calm myself down and have a smoke I needed one badly, and to apologize later, properly if she would let me.

And hope that she had not felt insulted, by my words, and actions, as I turned, she grabbed my arm, and pulled me back towards her, then she kissed me, gently but firmly, I just stood there, shocked, like a dumb ox, "it's okay" she whispered, "I have been feeling the same way myself, despite trying to hate you, your married, and ten years older, but whatever I did, just didn't work, I do really love you too, and I don't care, but like you dare not say so".

We just stood there, cuddling each other, the embrace was much more than each had hoped for, how long we stood there like that I don't know, time didn't exist. Eventually we parted and sat down on some boxes in a darkened corner, holding and caressing each other, we spoke for a long time, then we heard others coming into the store room, so we arranged to meet after work, me I really needed that cupper and smoke now more than ever.

I wanted to shout it out, but kept quiet, we could shout it later, in our own company, in private, when we met later, we decided to go to a motel, as she lived with her parents, after talking for a while, trying our best to sort out the problems, of our differences, like age, work, and life in general, then we caressed each other and made love, not the mad lust of youth, but a gentle kind of loving, for the sheer pleasure of being together, and feeling all the contours of each others body, in a gentle lasting love so pure in its touch that even now we often have tears, and just cling to each other until we feel calm again, we have minor problems to work out, but we meet as often as possible, until all is settled, this is how it will have to be, with me and my gentle love.

OUR UTOPIA

On waking up this morning, I thought that I should put pen to paper, so to speak, and record for all who may read it, like, future generations, of how we began in our Huaca, this is the name we gave our haven, an Inca word for holy place.

As later on the reader will find that the Incas do play a large part in our survival, a sort of history book, I suppose, something to record the start of our time in our Huaca, much like the beginning of time for us, but time starting within time itself.

This is an account of people brought together by a dream, a dream so real and strong in its incentive, that each individual gave up their way of life, to follow the dream, and the inexplicit urge to its ultimate conclusion.

I have recorded places, and people we met along the way, as some play a minor part.

For my part it started when I was looking through holiday brochures, sitting in my lounge, on a bright sunny day, with the sun shining in through the windows, and all was at peace, I rather fancied the Azores, and my wife agreed.

It was after this that the dreams started, at first the dream was a little, which I thought "was like any other dream, a fanciful whim, but the dream persisted, night after night, and more was unfolded before me, much like an episode of a serial drama" so after two months of the same dream, I spoke to my wife about it, and found that it was the same for her, one morning after about six months of the persistent dream, we knew what we had to do, but where to go, There was only a slight clue to us in our dreams, after much talking and discussion about this we had a plan, a drastic plan, giving up everything to follow a dream, we had no choice, it seemed the only way forward, before it drove us mad, I told my boss that I was "resigning my job, and moving to a new job in York" (which was about three hundred miles away,) so that no one, not even my best mates, whom I hated to leave or even less lie to, even for the first time, or our good neighbours, would not worry too much, if they never saw us again, sort of out of sight out of mind, this was our plan.

Dorothy went to the travel agents to book a walking tour of Europe for us, we had always been keen ramblers, and had walked many paths around the country, and not knowing how long our journey would take us, we had decided to conserve as much money as possible, by buying tin food, but not too much weight wise, and to buy other types of food in the country we were visiting at the time.

We put our house on the market at a knock down price for a quick sale, and telling our friends that we would send them post cards from the different countries that we visit, we could not tell them the real reason for going, they would think us nuts, and I wouldn't blame them either.

we had no ties, as we never had children something we never got round to, but we didn't mind, we were happy with each others company.

Finally the day came for us to depart, the ship sailed at two p.m. what a relief, on the morning of our departure we put on our haver sacks and stout walking shoes, with a spare pair tied to our packs, at last we were off.

Off to an adventure of who knows what, the last three months of waiting were over, and living at a boarding house, didn't suit us very much, I was getting touchy and moody.

But my wife, although anxious to be off like me, was more tactful and patient.

We walked through the town where we had spent so many years of our lives, and down to the station to purchase our one way tickets to Dover, we sat down to wait for the train, leaving this town wasn't too bad, just a little sadness, but now feeling more settled, in our walking gear, which we were more comfortable in, even though we may look a bit odd to some people especially me, with my battered old hat, but I liked it, and we were off on our adventure into the unknown at last.

Which was a great comfort to our poor bewildered and battered brains, especially after the last few months of persistent dreams, and the urge to go, seemed to overwhelm us.

Our first stop was Dover to catch a ferry to France, the crossing was uneventful, and we sat and talked to two brothers, Hayden and Aaron Taylor, who were on a day trip just for the sights, at Calais we said our good bye's and went our separate ways.

We took the road to Rouen, setting up our tent wherever we could find a spot, mostly in picnic areas, from Rouen we went onto Alencon, and then to Le Mons, at this point we wasn't sure were to go next, as we relied on our instincts and dreams for guidance, but always southwards, the walk wasn't too bad so far, as we were in no rush to go anywhere, we thought to go to Tours, especially as we were on a tour, so to speak.

In the morning off we set again, we didn't walk fast more like a stroll, which suited us, after covering about three miles a lorry pulled up at the roadside near us, and a gruff cockney voice called out, "wont a lift mates, ahm gahn dahn ta Toulouse" I thought "why not, I knew Dorothy would like his accent, she was into accents, and could copy some very well".

We joined him in the cab, and thanked him for stopping, we talked for a while, and told him "that we were on a walking tour of Europe, and that I kept a journal of our travels, I didn't know why at the time, but on reflection, I do now" when we stopped in Toulouse that night and climbed down from the cab, we thanked him again for the lift, "cheers Barry" we said, slightly dusty and engine oil smells everywhere, "na sa rite mates" he replied, and drove off in a cloud of dust and smoke, as for me "I would like to take a day of rest in Toulouse, just for a change" Dorothy thought it "a good idea" as well.

After spending a whole week in Toulouse looking over the town and countryside, we were well at ease, and well rested, the first time for a while, I had purchased a compass, a robust little thing I thought, but mainly for my own peace of mind, "I had a dream two nights ago, and needed to travel south, but not knowing north from south or east from west, only by guess work, my compass would come in very handy indeed".

We had decided to ride for a change instead of walking, so stowing our gear, we walked down to the bus depot to get one way tickets to Barcelona.

What a journey, hot, stuffy, dry, and dirty, dust got every where, and we were covered in sweat, I felt like I hadn't bathed for a month, not just two days non stop, when the bus stopped in Barcelona, us and other passengers that we had chatted to on the journey, headed for the nearest hotel, a bath and sleep were the first priorities,. On the list, and washing of clothes was the second item, next day refreshed again, we met up with the new friends that we had met on the bus as arranged, for a drink and a chat, just talking about every thing in general, Mary and Frank Newnes, with their children David and Janet.

John and Sue Dodd a young couple, Derek and Barbara Dorney, and their children, Hayley and Darrel, we were more like a coach party ourselves, we looked around Barcelona the rest of the day.

On the following morning we took the road, walking this time, To Valencia, walking and thumbing lifts, the journey wasn't so bad, at Valencia we had an urge to turn South west, good old compass, so we did, and made our way across country to Malaga, we always enjoyed the scenery, we enjoyed nature, this is an important place for us.

As this is where we first met Jeff, who became as a son to us, it was just before we reached the out skirts of Malaga, at a place named Isnaloz, near Loja, anyway, we had stopped for the night pitched the tent, and were cooking some eggs, beans and bacon, this was the wife's chore, as I intended to burn every thing, the kitchen was not a good place for me to be, "I could even burn water, so I'm told".

Most things were in the same pan, this saved on washing up and having to carry saucepans, when I heard foot steps behind me, turning round I heard a grating sort of voice ask, "got any to spare, I'm starving as well" "cheeky sod" I thought, but seeing he had a rucksack like us, and he was walking as well, I knew how he felt with the smell of cooking, "okay why not" I motioned him to sit, but the wife had already put more in the pan, we all ate hungrily with the food and coffee done, we felt more at ease, we chatted for a while, his name was Jeff Leigh, a blond six footer, quite muscular in build, dressed in khaki shorts, and a red shirt with stout walking boots, unlike me five feet six, slim built, and the wife, five feet four and cuddly, we both have brown hair.

We talked about what we were doing and where we were going sort of, we seemed to be doing and going the same way, "a kinsman" I thought, but did not ask, especially on our first meeting, we doused the fire and went to our tents for a good nights sleep, in the morning we were wakened by the smell of breakfast cooking, "eggs and fried bread lovely" I thought, I peeped out of the tent flap, and there was Jeff grinning, "come on lazy bones" I looked at my watch, six thirty in the morning, "me lazy, huh" I muttered, we had breakfast anyway, his cooking was good, most certainly better than mine, after breakfast, we sat and talked quite openly, as Jeff seemed to have something on his mind, and I was convinced that Jeff was a fellow traveler like us, searching, following instincts, I approached the subject cautiously, and his reply was astounding, like us "he had the dreams, but his journey always ended in Malaga, and not knowing why, he had been coming here for three years now, and this was to be his last time" as it was, in his words, "driving him nuts" until today there had been no change.

We told each other our stories, and decided to travel together as companions of whatever, and that I should still keep my journal, this seemed logical at least, I could see the relief on Jeff's face, just knowing that he wasn't the only one, who was bonkers, with dreams that urge you on.

We decided to go to Seville, and then on to Lisboa in Portugal, Jeff's knowledge of survival in the wilds certainly helped us on our journey, water from tree leaves, covered in a plastic bag overnight, was quite drinkable, we were amazed, saved carrying lots of water bottles, the trek across the mountains to Lisboa, was uneventful, just a long slog everyday, the scenery was nice though, and we stopped to watch some eagles, beautiful they are.

Finally we got to Lisboa, at Lisboa we decided to rest for a few days, our feet certainly needed it, in fact it was decided that a rest was required at every city or major town that we came across, as we were not in a hurry, just forever going onward compelled by an inexplicable urge.

We met an English family while out shopping, and asked them of any news, as we couldn't read the local paper, not knowing the language, they related the current events to us, we invited them to lunch with us as a thank you gesture, they were a family on holiday, Les and Vera with their children, Michael, Clair Tina and Dan we finished our meal paid for it, and said our farewells then left.

At Lisboa Jeff phoned his sister as always, to tell her "he would soon be home with some good news" it was decided to take a train to Madrid, and then the longest train ride we have ever been on, from Madrid to Paris, on the journey we talked with another family from England, just going home after a holiday, Rod and Lillian, with their children, Tasha, and Phil, they were all a bit sad at going home.

they had enjoyed the holiday, it appears to us all, that the only reason for us coming this far on our journey, was just to meet Jeff, "who knows" From Paris we caught another train to Calais, then a boat to Dover, and a train again to London, where Jeff's sister Maree would meet us, and drive to their home in Devon.

We chatted to her all the way there, sometimes Dorothy and Maree talked about woman's things, while us men discussed our next step to take, Maree was delighted about us meeting Jeff, being of the same mind, with the same instincts and shared his dreams as well, Maree I noticed was slim built, about five feet six tall, fair haired, also quite hardy in character, and engaged to Rob, an engineer who worked oversees for an oil company, he had just gone back for a two year stint, to make enough money to get married on.

Upon reaching their home, which was in Bampton, Devon, we unpacked our rucksacks, had tea and I tried some zider, whew strong stuff, I barely remember going to bed, their home was a three bed semi, but quite spacious, well furnished and airy, the décor matched their personalities.

In the morning Jeff and I spoke of our dreams and feelings, as we did each morning, to decide what to do or where to go, after a couple of days Jeff had a notion "to go to America" we discussed this and it was agreed "yes we would" having the same inclination, on telling Maree of our decision, she asked "if she could come" to this we all readily agreed, and with arrangements to be made for our passage to America, and getting all the equipment we might need on our next step of the journey, all this took six weeks, after the six weeks had elapsed, we were off again.

Maree had written to Rob to explain all this, so that there was no problem there, we took a train to London, to catch our ship bound for New York, the crossing wasn't so bad, we met other passengers, talked and dined with them, a family emigrating to America, for a better life, Douglas and Catherine Clemons, with their children, Kathleen, Mary and Dorothy, they were okay at sea, but not being a good sailor myself, if we hit bad weather, I was seasick, the others enjoyed the trip, New York appeared I for one was thankful, terra firma at last.

We were impatient to continue our journey, after resting on the crossing, and going through customs as visitors, we met up outside and went to look for a car to buy, eventually we found one, a second hand battered Chevrolet.

We thought "to drive down to Colombia, in south Carolina".

We reached Colombia on a wet and windy day, so "it was decided to book into a motel for a weeks rest, and sort ourselves out" but first a bath and some clean clothes after four days, we knew that we had to go on to Mexico, so I plotted a course on the map, this was my job, and off we went.

But as we neared Atlanta, the car broke down, we nursed it into car dealers, and brought another one, a station wagon was the type, we continued our journey onto Birmingham, then to Shreveport, in Houston, and from there to San Antonio, by now we were all fed up with motoring, and stopped to rest for a while.

A few days really, we brought another car as ours was playing up a bit, in conclusion, I thought "that second hand cars just didn't last very long on these sort of journeys" well rested and at ease, we found that we had another problem, Jeff and I wanted to go different ways, so we talked as always, Maree had a good idea, "a course midway" this agreed and this we did, after plotting a course for Lubbock in New Mexico, we set off, we went from Lubbock to Roswell, and onto El

Paso, at El Paso I and Dorothy decided that to the rest of the world we would be dead, this we had talked about for some time now, having drawn all our money from a bank in Houston, and closed the account, I knew that no one would be looking for us, this Jeff did by sending a cable to our nephew, the only living relative, we were killed when we fell over a precipice while climbing in the Mexican hills, and that we had been cremated, for health reasons.

A certificate was obtained for a sum of cash, from a back street doctor, all this done, it was the final break from friends and family, we felt a little sad, and a pang of regret for the first time since setting off, some six months ago, my eyes moistened, as I thought of the sorrow the news would bring to some, but I resolved it had to be done.

I felt better after a while, as we rested in El Paso, and looked over the town, Maree had sent a cable to Rob, she had enough of traveling, and was badly missing Rob, so having bought a plane ticket to Dallas, she would then fly onto Houston, where Rob would meet her in a few days time, we had not flown anywhere since our journey began, "I think we have to travel the hard way, at this point in time, but didn't know why" we said "goodbye" to Maree at the airport, and thanked her for her company and kindness, and as Dorothy and I agreed, we gave Maree an envelope with three thousand dollars in it, to help with the wedding expenses.

We were glad to help.

Knowing that we would never see her again, and visa versa, with moist eyes, I told Jeff where we would be camping outside of town, and would wait for his return, as we knew him by now, he would want to say his goodbye to his sister in private, knowing that they may never see each other again, and that he would need a few days on his own to come to terms with the loss of his sister and confidant of many years.

As we were having breakfast some six days later, wondering where Jeff was, and talking about the next move, someone spoke behind me, this startled me, making me spill my coffee, I jumped up and turned around, there was Jeff, I grabbed and hugged him, I was glad to see him again, he had come home, called the wife excitedly, she came quickly, "ah at last" she exclaimed, giving him a hug, she was glad to see him as well, after he had finished eating, washed and shaved, he was scruffy and unshaven.

He said he "hadn't shaved for a week, or hardly eaten" in his remorse he had neglected himself, "got drunk for two days but now sober, and better" "good" I thought "now to the task in hand, where to go" we rested the rest of the day, just lazed around talking and decided to go onto Santiago, in the morning we set off as usual, after driving for about two hours a car was seen by the roadside, we stopped to ask if help was needed, and it certainly was.

We chatted to them while Jeff fixed their fan belt, which wasn't very good, and put a new one on, they were Mick and Alison Wakefield, about sixty years old, both portly in build, just touring in latter years, we agreed to drive along with them as company and mechanic, just in case, we stopped at Chihuahua, that night and met up again in the morning to continue our journey, we passed through Ciudad Camargo and onto Torreon, but before we reached Torreon, Mick saw four hitch hikers and stopped to pick them up.

twins Toni and Terri Lawson, they were about five feet six tall, with brown hair, twenty five years old, slim built, the other two were Lynn and John Haugh, a couple in their thirties, about five feet eight, blond and slim, all were dressed up for hiking, boots shorts and all the gear seemed to be the in thing these days.

Toni and Terri rode with us, John and Lynn rode in the other car, this way we continued on, Torreon came and went, and we traveled onto Zacatecas, when we got there Mick was not feeling well, John drove their car down to Guadalajara, as the Wakefield's had decided to fly home from there to Cincinnati, their home town, while John and Lynn would drive the car home for them, as their holiday would be nearing its end by the time they arrived in Cincinnati.

On the journey we had chatted to the girls, and Jeff had encroached on our quest, he found out that they were also like us, on an urge always going southwards, we were a mixed bunch of people on the same journey, at Guadalajara we bade the Wakefield's and Haughs a "bon voyage" the twins had elected to come with us, we then departed for Puebla, our next port of call, and then onto Guatemala town, here we stopped as is our want, we rested for a few days, but the urge was stronger now, and we all grew restless, so we went to San Miguel, and onto San Jose, here we stopped for a rest again, as we were all happy, we knew that we were on the right track of our destination.

After San Jose we arrived at last in Balboa, in the early afternoon, tomorrow we decided we would cross the Panama Canal, and go onto Medellin, but Medellin seemed to be in the height of its holiday season, and as our car was clapped out, we bought yet another one, and drove down into Ecuador, to a place named Guavaquil, where we rested for a few days, constant driving was taking it's toll on us.

We mingled with the holiday makers, but we didn't seem to fit in, so we decided to move on, we took the coast road to Huermey, and we met a group of travelers, like us, all dusty and dirty, whose car had given up for good, a family named Dennis, Joe and his wife Debbie, with their children, Billie, Georgina and Jack, we offered to take them to Lima, so off we set in our over crowded estate car, I'm sure this was Illegal.

Four hours later we arrived at Lima, and drove to a place where they were to meet a cousin of the Dennis's named Aimee, when we arrived at the meeting place in Lima, and I first saw Aimee, I knew, I knew, but had to wait to find out.

I talked with the others of our group, they agreed, it was the look in the eyes, dressed only in a shirt, jeans and sandals, a dead give away, as Jeff and I had discovered awhile ago, Joe introduced us, Aimee was slim, with long dark hair, about five feet eight tall, with bright brown eyes, I think Aimee knew as well, by the look of surprise at seeing us.

We all got settled into a motel, cleaned up and met up for a meal, paid for by Joe, for our kindness, ten of us, after having eaten, we said our good bye's to the Dennis's, and invited Aimee to join us, at Mutacana, where we would be going tomorrow, it is a small town a few miles away, and we would be there for a week or so, to rest and to plan our next move, this was Toni's idea.

next day in Mutacana Toni and Terri looked around the town, buying the odd things that women like, while Jeff and I checked over the equipment and supplies, Dorothy unassuming as ever, did her chores then went to town to meet the girl's, and get her things.

After checking all the supplies for the next part of the journey, Jeff and I went to town to purchase the supplies needed, the Peruvian people were quite friendly, and eager to supply anything for a few dollars, being low economy was good for us, we purchased a couple of mules, as we needed to carry a lot more food this time, and the services of a guide, in exchange for our car, bartering seemed to be the thing, and Jeff was a past master at it.

After all was done, when I checked, we only had eight thousand dollars left to last, Aimee joined us on the fifth day, after saying goodbye to her cousins, they were okay now, we talked at length with Aimee each telling her their own different stories, of how we met and why we are together, Aimee told us her tale, she "had been in Peru for two years now, searching for who knows what" I wondered, the urge to go somewhere was the same as ours, I put it to the vote, all agreed unanimously, so Aimee joined our happy band of wanderers, the night before we set off again, I reflected at what had passed in the time since we first left England, these last few months, all told, our sort of rules, but more like guide lines, which we all must agree upon, as and when the situation arises, our talks with each other in the mornings, and when anyone was disheartened, which we all were at times, the others would encourage them to go on, and the frustrations would soon pass, cheered on by our companions.

We were a small bunch of people that left Matucana that morning, two men four women, a guide and two mules, we climbed up into the mountains, the way was hard and slow with the mules, and we had to rest often, at last we came to a village named Tomas, and here our guide had to leave us, as agreed with Jeff, who gave him the car keys, he was quite happy, but we knew that now we didn't need a guides services anymore, because instincts and gut feelings had taken over again, we said "goodbye" to our guide, he was a colourful Peruvian, as all Peruvians are, also steeped in traditions and belief's.

We set off again after a few days rest, we walked along a ridge of the mountains following only gut feelings and instincts, we stopped at several places along the way, wondering if this was it, but no, after a couple of days, on we went, but knowing that we were so close helped a lot, we had been wandering the mountains for three months now.

The ache of the urge always onwards, would make tempers short, when this happened, we stopped and rested till all were calm again, this was another rule entered into my third diary, we passed lake Titicaca, and rested a few days with the local Aymara Indians that lived nearby, replenished our food supply, then trekked across country to see the drawings in the Nasca dessert, then we headed back into the mountains again to see the city of Machu Picchu.

We also saw the Inca sacred stone to the sun god, called the Intihuatana, and the volcanic peak, Sava Sava, "why we had to see all these things, I still do not know" one hot stuffy afternoon after crossing a flat topped peak, looking across a valley, Toni spotted a cave with a flat ledge jutting out over the brim, that we had passed on the way down, it seemed to catch the eye, we all seemed excited at the find, at the time, not knowing why, although we were tired and weary, we all wanted to climb back up, it seemed to draw you to it.

No one else had seen it on the way down, because the ledge hid it from view, it was decided "to be patient, mainly because we were tired, and to climb back up being tired would have been foolish and dangerous, best wait till morning it's safer when we are rested" morning came a bright day as usual among the mountains, so high above the rest of the world, climbing back up was an arduous task, as the air was rarified at this height, and breathing came in gasps with the effort of using a lot of muscle power, Jeff climbed first, being the younger and fittest, then he threw down ropes to help the rest of us climb up, this task took all day, to get us and our equipment on top of the flat peak again.

We waited until the next day before doing any more, in the morning we tied ropes around huge boulders, to act as anchors, Jeff went first down to the ledge, holding himself at an angle on the rope, he could just see into the cave mouth, then he climbed back up, which was awkward as the ledge was only three feet wide, and the edges were sharp.

We agreed that all should be in the cave before exploring it's depth, "we wait until tomorrow" was mentioned, and all agreed, as there were many grass torches to be made, to last a long time in the cave, which Jeff had said was deep, he was the most impatient, but tomorrow would come soon enough, I slept restlessly that night, as did the others, I could hear them talking, laying there, waiting for day light.

I was fully awakened by a yell, rushing outside of our tent just as the girls emerged from theirs.

"What's up" everyone asked each other, Terri went to fetch Jeff, but found him missing, we rushed to the edge of the plateau, I lowered a lighted torch on a rope down towards the ledge, and saw a pair of eyes looking up, "help" came a small voice, "you bloody idiot" I cursed him for his impatience, I tied a rope around my waist and went down to help Jeff onto the ledge, giving him the other rope, before climbing back up, and waited for Jeff to follow, he had missed his footing in the dark, and slipped off the ledge, "twit" I muttered to him as he reached us.

But glad that it was nothing worse than a few cuts bruises and hurt pride, daylight was approaching by now, we had breakfast and prepared for the day ahead, but not before mother had a few chosen words with Jeff about his stupidity, my wife was called mother and I father, because of our age I suppose, we didn't mind, they were like our children to us.

This the others had decided amongst themselves, and we accepted it, after breakfast was done, we prepared to climb down to the cave, my arms still ached from last night's rescue, so I elected to go last.

Terri being the slightest of us was to go first, and throw lighted torches into the cave mouth, in case of unseen dangers, this done she swung herself into the cave, after what seemed an eternity, she called back, "it's okay, come on down" we dropped the other ropes down, Jeff was first, as Terri had to catch his rope to pull him in, one by one we reached the cave floor, with a spare rope tied to our waist, so we could be pulled in by the others.

The cave was well lit by our torches, we started to search it, it was about ten feet wide, ten feet high, and thirty feet deep, is this all I thought, why all the excitement, and we sat down to rest, one torch by a corner was flickering madly, like on a windy day, I wiped away the dust on the stone face of the cave with my hand, and found a cut in the wall, it was then that I noticed the wall was flat.

I took off my shirt, to use as a duster, after wiping off the entire wall, amid the strange looks and words of, "are you mad" chocking on the dust a wall appeared "aha, me mad never" everyone was getting quite excited by now, it was built in the Inca style of wall much like a jigsaw puzzle, like the other Inca dwellings we had seen before in these mountains, where the torch flame was flickering, I put my knife into the gap between the blocks, and clearing the dirt from around the shape of the blocks where my knife blade could go in, but in my haste, I broke the blade of my knife, and cursed myself for my impatience.

By now some of the others had also started, on the other side of the cave, and I sat down with the wife, to wait until the others had finished the task, she whispered to me, "never mind, we'll soon find out what it is" a patient person is my wife, and sensible too, not like me, the shape they uncovered was arch like, assuming it was a door we all tried to move it, but to no avail, and we all sat down on the floor a bit dejected, after all the work, after awhile Aimee suggested "a lever" but what, we talked into the night, and decided to go to the nearest village or town, to purchase what tools we could with what little money we had left, "as we decided by now, win or bust, we would move the stone".

The following day we set off, after having built a stone mound with a stick in it, and a piece of Jeff's red shirt as a flag pole marker, I had to go by compass and by time of walking, as these were the only references as to where we were, we walked due east for about four hours, when I spotted a Peruvian dwelling we had seen before, which was on my home made map, "good" I thought, so now I can work out a route to Tacna.

When we reached Tacna a week later, more a rabble than the sightseers, which we were supposed to be, all dirty, dusty and ragged, we set about the task of finding the tools and clothes that we needed, and could find cheap among the locals, we got a pickaxe, a shovel, a small axe, and a hammer, I managed to persuade an old local to part with an iron bar that had a flat on one end, for a few dollars, this all done, except some more supplies.

The girls wanted a few days to relax, and look around, so we did, dressed more like locals now, with our new clothes, even despite any urge to hurry back, "but what the hell

I thought, the caves not going anywhere is it" Jeff sent a letter to Maree and Rob to explain everything, three days later Aimee brought two young friends into camp, she had known and worked with them on different sites in Peru, their names were Sophie Watt, slim sun tanned, fair haired, dressed much like us, and with her back pack, she was Aimee's age thirty five, she was also an archaeologist, who had been in Peru for some years, and Lucy Winn, another archaeologist, she was short and chubby, brown haired, she had been with Sophie for three years now, and still looking for what? Just like we were, it's the ever searching look that gives you away; both had been excavating Inca sites.

Aimee explained that Sophie and Lucy could supply us with answers as they were quite knowledgeable on the subject of Inca buildings, culture, and religion, Sophie also spoke Peruvian quite well, we spoke for a whole day, on many things they were really interested, as Aimee said they would be.

I suspected that Aimee might have told them about us by the looks to each other as we talked, that night Aimee told both the girls of our find, while the rest of us just sat and listened, Sophie and Lucy wanted to come with us, as I thought they would.

After Aimee's assurance of silence from them, it was agreed, having packed the following morning, we set off for the cave, we reached our marker at the top of the cave, after losing the way twice, my fault, I'm not the best navigator, but I was the only one with the map, compass, and the time of walking, a safety precaution we made, and I also found another route to the cave, much by error, a quicker one, a whole day quicker, which was good.

I had noticed the tired look in my wife's eyes, all this trecking around was taking it's toll on us, I felt the same sometimes, but she never once complained, bless her, the morning after our arrival back at the site, we climbed down into the cave mouth with lots of torches and some paraffin lamps, after examining the wall, Sophie said it was Inca, she also thought it to be a door, and it would be pivoted in the middle, this Lucy agreed, and it would swivel round when opened, we used the bar one side nothing happened, so we tried the other side, it moved, it moved, I danced on the spot, in excitement, much like a child stamping it's feet, shouting "yeah, yeah" American style, much to everyone's amazement, and amusement, this I had picked up from the twins.

Having calmed myself down, and with the others chatting wildly, Jeff and I put all our might upon the lever, which started to bend, but the door started to open, about a foot, all hands were pulling at the door now, just enough to squeeze through and push from the other side, until the gap was a good three feet wide, it was daylight, I was disappointed, I'd expected darkness, on the other side, "why I don't know".

We all got through onto a ledge about ten feet square, with steps cut into the rock, leading down to the valley floor, a valley much like the one behind us, we were all a little dejected, "all this just to get from valley to valley" Terri said, voicing our thoughts.

But our disappointment was short lived, as we later found out, "at the moment I think that we were pessimists, especially after such a long time of searching".

On reaching the valley floor we decided to look over the valley, but keep together as a group, not knowing what to expect next, the valley as we discovered over the next few weeks, was three miles long, half a mile wide, we paced it out roughly, with a river running through one side, the water was two feet deep and cold.

The walls of the valley were too sheer to climb on the inside, and the peeks too ragged to climb on the outside, the ends of the valley were the same, completely blocking us in, the land was very fertile, not having been touched for a very long time.

Several trees were around and lots of grass, a building stood at one end with six rooms plus a large room in the middle, a temple stood next to this, the size of a house, "nothing grand by Inca standards" I'm told.

All doors were of the swivel type, in the temple was a black and charred stone slab, and a black and grimy hole in the ceiling, Sophie told us "it was probably a place of worship, and of offerings to their gods.

We also found that in the river gold ore was abundant, "is this the valley if the Incas that the Spanish invaders never found, the mysterious valley of gold, the Eldorado, that men have been searching for, for centuries" I voiced this question, but was only greeted by shrugs.

"Who knows"? And the door was well disguised, we only found it by chance, but why was it abandoned, we found no human skeletons anywhere, or grave markers, after exploring the entire valley, Dorothy and I decided that this was it, our Shangri-La, our heaven.

When we announced this to the others, everyone, including Sophie and Lucy had elected to stay as well, as the urge to move on had ceased, along with the dreams, only feelings of peace and tranquility were apparent.

"Had some celestial being guided us here, given us our dreams, and the urge to seek and find this place, and for us to be the keepers of such a realm, I didn't know or care, here we were and here we were staying, and that was that".

We had been in the valley for two months now, and rations were getting low, we went to the nearest village to buy supplies, about eight days each way, then return to the valley to plan for the future, we talked at length about the way we spend our lives in our valley called Huaca, after the Incas, our ways were to be simple, without the contradictions of different religions, we were to keep two Christian festivals, but would be at a different time, as we had no way of knowing what month it was.

Since our arrival all watches had been discarded, time was not important anymore, we were a happy family residing here, and no one was tired anymore.

Just happy, plans were made for growing corn, planting new trees, and even digging a fish pond, to help with the diet, but there were no fish here, the river coming in as an underground stream, and going out the same, "but what fish to catch in other valley rivers"?.

Only time would tell if they survive, but as winter was in the outside world, and we would have to wait till it was over, having dug a pond three feet deep twenty feet long and twenty feet wide, at one end of the valley, we were satisfied.

"A nice big pond" I thought "good" winter in the valley was quite mild, sheltered as it was, from the raging wind and rain, winter passed and we had made an oven of stones, for melting gold, and copper, there was a huge pile of copper ore, brought all the way from the copper mines, a good distance away, to make whatever we fancied, jewellery, tools but I'm not sure if copper tools would be any good, time would tell.

We decided to go back to Tacna, and buy every thing we could, for our survival, Sophie said that she "had eight hundred pounds in the bank, which she put at our disposal, as she was staying, she had no further use for money, she would send a telegram to her parents telling them that she had joined an expedition and did not know when she would be back" as she explained her younger years to us, we knew she would not be missed.

The twins were okay as they had no parents and had wandered around America for a time, with friends Maizie and Charlie and kai who had gone another way, before meeting us, Lucy wanted to stay and be second cook with mother, she liked that, so that was okay, Aimee wasn't sure yet, so it was just left at that, and for the time being all bridges were considered burnt.

When we finally reached Tacna, the girls had their lists of articles to purchase, Sophie had her special list of items, while Jeff and I had ours, we each had separate lists of items so as not to arouse any suspicions, probably we were over cautious, but this is what we wanted, we waited for the others at a pre arranged site, where we had pitched our tents on the way down.

It took a whole week before we were all assembled with our goods and livestock, all young animals, our list was varied, we had ten chickens in a cage, a sack of maize seed, one of potatoes, a bag of salt, one of sugar, of rice and flour, two goats, three sheep, and two Acunyas, one male one female, to carry loads as well, Sophie wrote to her two cousins Ashlie and Danielle and Gracie to tell them the same story as she told her parents.

Jeff wrote to Maree to explain everything, knowing that she and Rob would be pleased with the news, off we set a motley crew, a bit like a wagon train of the old wild west, on the way back nearing our turning point, a lone tent was spotted, on checking the tent it was found empty, it was probably someone's base camp, "we decided to camp for the night as well" at sunrise as we were just gathering everything together, Terri said that she thought she heard a faint cry of help in the night, but wasn't sure, we decided to look at least, as these mountains were treacherous indeed, we spread out in pairs to look, but no more than a half hour or so's walk, lest we get lost ourselves.

The first half day nothing was found, we next went in other directions, Toni and Aimee called us on their whistles, three blasts.

Which is the best way of calling anyone in these mountains, the shrill sound can be heard for miles, Jeff blew a single blast on his whistle to let them know we had heard them, on reaching them we saw a middle aged man, fair haired, about five feet ten tall, slim waisted, but broad in the shoulders, he was unconscious, Toni and Aimee had checked him over, and found apart from cuts and bruises everywhere, he also had a broken leg, he looked like he had fallen or tumbled down a rocky face, and was dragging himself back to his camp site, but had passed out with the pain, no mean feat over rocky terrain, a tough fellow indeed.

We made a makeshift stretcher, which Jeff and I carried him back to the camp on, we washed and tended to his cuts and bruises, and fixed his broken leg with tree branches, then tied the two legs together to help prevent movement, all seemed okay, now we needed a nice cup of coffee, this done the girls searched his belongings for his name, it was Olf Svenson, a Norwegian.

Olf started muttering regaining some sort of consciousness, then unconscious again, he was in a bad state of health, which gave us a dilemma, "what do we do with him now" I pondered the question, "does one of us stay here with him, possibly for two to three months, or do we take him with us, our haven was the nearest place, only two days away, as the journey was eight days each way" this we did, a slower two days, three really, but we had to be very careful for Olf's sake, we all knew a bit of first aid, but mother was a nurse in working life.

At the cave entrance Aimee went first to go in and fetch mother and Lucy, so as to be ready when we got Olf into the valley, Olf was taken straight to the house, while we continued to get the animals and goods into the cave, with a makeshift hoist, a triangle of poles and ropes, then to the valley floor, this took a whole week, we were happy with being able to be self sufficient, and a few days rest were needed, being so busy this last week, I had failed to notice that while we had been away, Toni the talented one of us, had painted a picture on the wall in the large room, the colour and likeness of my wife, it was very good, "it will take quite a while" she said "but, we will all have our portraits painted on the walls".

I'm not sure what was used as paint pigments of sorts, I suppose, but that's an artists secret, so I'm told, I was very pleased anyway.

Sophie and Lucy had been deciphering some of the carvings, there were references as to the place of the mines of Tayopa, but this is something to think about later on. "Maybe the younger ones with adventure still in them, might go to look for the mines, or even where the fabled city of Atlanta was, before being destroyed by the ocean of storms, at a place called Helike, of the Minoans, and the cuppa cappa a ritual, of sacrificing young female virgins to the volcano god Amputo, who knows" we let the animals roam free, until we could build walls to separate animals from the fields, plenty of rocks around for walls, we made some bellows, for getting the fire hot enough to melt the gold ore, after we had crushed it up, to make melting easier, and for other metals we want to melt.

The work was hard going, but we were getting there, we made each field about an acre in size, cleared it of stones and sometimes big rocks, which we used to build the field walls with, although only about three feet high they were enough to separate each field, we plan to plant alternately.

So that as one crop is finished, the other one is growing, to help maintain a continuous source of food.

Olf`s leg had healed, but he had a slight limp, which he didn't mind at all, with his and the girls help as well, they worked as hard as us men, most times more than me, we were getting there, I thought now was the time to go and get our fish for the pond, and to see if they survive the next few months.

Off we went using a part of a tent full of holes for a net, but carrying them back was the worst problem, in a homemade tank of branches and a tent, we managed with a struggle, and hoping for the best, the girls picked up the fish that jumped out during the bumpy journey back, we got them to the pond and tipped them in, twenty lovely trout.

We made paddles on a pole which turned with the force of the water, this fed the pond, several more were made for irrigating the fields, it was during this time that Sophie and Lucy had translated a lot more of the carvings, more like a record book or account of events.

Like the reason for the Nasca desert drawings, and what the Inca sacred stone called the Intihuatana was really for, the Incas were also a race that glorified in war and religion, barbaric at least I would say, and their last king Kinnichi, is mentioned as dying of the disease that killed off a vast majority of the nation.

"That's probably why this place was abandoned! I thought, the jade ornaments we found the women wore, the effigy pots were used every day, we didn't use the quipu, knotted ropes for counting, as there was nothing to count, and we didn't bother to count months either, just the days, with seven stones, so that we could rest at weekends, so to speak, anyone could rest anytime if they wished, there were no hard and fast rules for working.

Mainly we just got on with the tasks in hand, waiting for another winter to pass, although winter in the valley wasn't bad at all quite mild in fact, sheltered as it was from the raging wind, some rain we got, but t was hot in the summer.

So we celebrated Easter at the beginning of summer, like a spring festival, and Christmas at the beginning of winter, as these were the only two seasons that were apparent here.

We had been here for about two years now, we got the ceiling and walls washed down at last, to make the house more habitable, like a spring clean, we also built a toilet block, with constant running water, with one of our wheels, and two showers, I had an idea to take Olf back to civilization, after swearing him to secrecy about our place.

but I was worrying needlessly, he wanted to stay, as he and Toni had laid claim to each other, and being thick I just didn't see it, everyone else knew, but not me, a meeting was called as usual, and Olf was invited to stay, he said "he would serve as best he could, but he wanted to tell us all about himself first, in short he had grown up and worked on his fathers farm, all his life until his father died, his mother having passed away many years before, and he had sold the farm and intended to see the world" his knowledge of farming would be very useful indeed.

After much talking it was decided that I as father would perform the wedding ceremony of Olf and Toni, and then one last trip to Tacna, the wedding was a simple affair, conducted in the temple with their vows nothing more than your name and I do, "what else was needed"?.

Spoken over a Quartz skull that we had found there, but was only to be used for blessings, christenings, marriages, and funerals, at other times it was covered up.

O n reaching Tacna, for the umpteenth time and maybe the last, we searched around for anything that maybe of any use to us, especially if it made life easier, I found a couple of old cast iron pots, which I thought might be better for melting down the gold or copper ore, the twins spent a couple of days going round and chatting to the tourists they had met, to find out how the world was, Claire, Rebecca, Hanna, Shaun and Barry, then related the news to the rest of us, seems the world was in a recession, Olf had found some books on smelting.

And a very useful tool called an adze, Jeff was not without being useful either, he had got a vee shaped plough blade, very useful indeed, a small axe, and some grapes, "we eat the grapes but keep the pips, to grow our own" he said, he also brought a variety of small items for the women folk.

"Trust him" I thought, collecting ourselves together we headed back home, trying to be careful with the vegetable plants that I had got, the lemon tree sapling, and two coffee tree saplings as well that Olf got.

When we arrived home, Jeff and Olf started to gather rocks, which were abundant here, to block up the cave mouth, so as to disguise it even more, the idea was to make it look just like any other cliff face, with rocks cemented in with mud, to dry as hard as cement, a good effect, but before finally starting the wall, one really final trip to Tacna, then seal ourselves in for good.

In Tacna, Jeff went to sell the gold at a back street dealer we used, a lot of gold this time, we got two thousand dollars, so now we could get anything that could be useful for our survival, and to make it easier, we kept in pairs, and went our different ways, me and Jeff, went and bought two adult donkeys, and two young ones, a male and female, for breeding as well as working, they were a small breed, but sturdy, and two donkey carts, with small but decent wagon type wheels, and a couple of spare wheels.

Olf and Toni got two boxes of nails, a hammer, a bow saw, an ordinary saw, two spades, and two shovels, I watched a local woman spinning the wool, ready to be woven on the loom, which I looked at, and I copied it into my note book, to be made later, the twins bought back to the campsite, a small axe, four metal buckets, tape measure, another adze, cooking pots of various sizes, and two frying pans.

we took a donkey and cart to get a sack of Papa Amarillo, (potatoes) two rolls of chicken wire, a sack of rice, and sack of flour, then we had a day of rest, but Jeff, Olf and me we went and had a look around, while the girls rested, we got a small barrel of Pisco, (Peruvian brandy,) four cane flutes, a guitar, we thought that "some of the talented ones might play them" crate of wine, pair of binoculars, sack of coffee beans, and two forks sometimes better for digging, on the way back to camp we also bought a small spinning wheel, we bought a few clothes, then we were broke, we opened a couple of bottles that night, just to celebrate a little, tomorrow we would be heading back home again.

The journey back was easier, we had put our rucksacks on the carts, instead of being weighed down, I was a little nervous on the way back, I kept checking with the binoculars for anyone trailing us, didn't see any though.

Just me, it took an extra three days to get every thing into the valley, the animals being the worse.

On the final day of finishing the wall in the cave mouth, two mud covered figures came to the house, we made them wash in the river fully clothed, apparently there had been a mud fight, to celebrate the finish, and they bathed amid much laughter.

"boys will be boys" I thought, mother told them off of course, and they had to wash the clothes properly afterwards, while we watched, there was still more work to be done, like the irrigation ditches for the fields, digging out the gold ore, and ways to get water to the house.

And many more little things, like a wheel to smash the corn then we throw it into the air for the slight breeze that is always here, summer or winter, this would blow the chaff towards a tent spread out, and this we would give to the animals and chickens as feed, a mill to grind the corn into flour, hopefully all courtesy of the water.

And a interchangeable arm, with the brandy barrel to make butter and cheese, hopefully.

One hot day about the time of finishing the walls, I realized that my clothes were getting tighter, on mentioning this to Jeff, who said "it was probably our rib cages growing, as our lungs had to expand to take in more air at a time, to compensate for the low oxygen atmosphere, as he had the same problem, and had spoken with the girls about it, was the same with them as well".

I agreed, "High in these mountains, it most probably was".

We were working away at the far end of the valley, digging the irrigation ditches, to get ready for planting, when mother came along in a donkey cart, having taken a day off for a change, just to see how we were doing; she had not been to this end, since our arrival here.

The cart saved a six mile walk, and was quicker, the young donkeys trot along quite well, at a steady pace, the cart gave me an idea, a plank of wood, to go across, as a seat, it's not much, but better than sitting inside the cart, the seat would have to be moveable, so we could still use it for work, if needed, other times it would be mothers cart.

All readily agreed to this idea, we are now a bit like living on a desert island, but for now we are content, away from the hurly burly, greed and scorn of the outer world.

While we live in peace and contentment in our valley.

OUR HUACA.

REBELS

We were being chased by the soldiers of the regime, but we split up to make things harder for them to capture us.

We the revolutionaries had fought the regimes armies but overrun by numbers had fled, I was running down side streets, ducking and diving laser fire, and firing back until my gun ran out.

I turned a corner running as fast as I could, then froze in my tracks, as I heard a hundred rifles being readied to fire, I had run into a patrol, and as I threw down my gun I swore "bastards, just my bloody luck" all I got from the soldiers was laughter, "your lucks not in today, is it scum" said the officer in charge, as he hit me in the face knocking me to the ground.

My hands were tied behind my back, and two soldiers marched me to a holding camp, this camp is where everyone is taken, to find out where they are to be sent, hard labour in an outpost was my fate, that was my sentence, no trial of course, I was a rebel.

And with my fellow captives I was put in a line, there were several rows of people, male and female, all waiting to be shipped out in floaters to various destinations.

There were us the rebels, and various mixed groups, and the not so bright, which were in a row next to ours, "'I'm going to get away if I can" I told one of my comrades, "don't be stupid, you'll get shot" he said, I just winked at him, and slipped into the not so bright line.

These people were for doing menial tasks; you could see them every where, in their khaki overalls with a white circle painted on back and front, "no mistaking them"

I thought, but by joining them might give me a chance to escape if I acted dumb, as nobody check's whose who at this stage, you were just put in rows and shipped out.

As we were herded into a floater my comrade in arms whispered "good luck".

We were then taken to another camp, after a days journey chained up in a floater I was glad to get out of the floater and have my chains removed, we were given khaki overalls with the circles on, then given our work tasks, I with three others were given the pig compound to clean then feed them.

the pig food had to be collected from the rear of the cook house, the soldiers didn't bother us very much, maybe it was the smell, which was just as well, at first it was awful, it made me feel sick, but I had to stick it out to escape, and didn't notice it so much after a couple of weeks, especially as our living quarters were a couple of spare pig sty's.

one day they made us clear a space at the end of the compound, take down an old building bring it into the compound and erect it, "your new luxury house to live in" they said laughing.

The soldiers were a cruel lot, and sadistic, the worst kind of people I've ever met.

although we didn't get the beating's the others got we still got verbal abuse, and lots of it, they wouldn't come near us, I didn't mind not one bit, but was determined more than ever to escape, and wipe the smile off their faces.

As more pigs arrived we had to work harder, now there were only two of us, the other two being taken away to do other duties, as the camp was filling up, with more trainees, you could see them practicing and getting kicked if they got anything wrong, they were ruled by fear.

I had been keeping my eyes and ears open all this time listening to bits of gossip, while doing the daily chores.

I was getting to be quite an expert thief, nicking anything I could from the camp, especially if it aided my escape plan, which was to dress up as a soldier and walk out past the guards, just like anyone else.

a bold plan but I had to try, going out the back way was probably useless anyway, it was the training area, forest and rough terrain as far as you could see, who knows how far, the only other option was through the dog compound, a large area where they the army kept their dogs.

They roamed free in this area, even the soldiers avoided this place, I think that they were only there to deter deserters, I had seen one once, caught and thrown in only to be torn to pieces, while your platoon were made to watch.

"Ugh" it made me feel sick, but I have heard them since, and I still cringe at the sound of a man screaming as he dies, while being torn apart alive by dogs, as vicious as their masters.

Desertion seems to be quite common among the new conscripts, who wants to join up anyway, most are caught even in the training area, if you don't get drowned in the swamps first, which is preferable, as their fate is always the same, dogs meat, in fact if you are found guilty of any crime these days, even some civilians, you were of course, dog meat.

I don't think they feed them on anything else, but human flesh, so being very cautious is a wise move, I managed to steal a pair of boots, two pairs of socks, a beret and a belt so far.

some poor sods got a kicking for losing his gear I bet, all these things I kept in the roof space, wrapped in polythene, to keep out the smell of the pigs, "couldn't have that smell giving me away could I".

but at this rate it will take me about a year to escape, unless I found a better way, and I was getting impatient to get out, it took me another two weeks to pinch a pair of trousers, the badges were no trouble, I nicked them when the blokes were in the shower block, one night, avoiding the sentry robots was always risky, but somehow I did it.

now I needed scissors to cut my hair, as it was a little long for a soldier, and a razor to shave with, and as I would have to go into a barrack room to get them from a soldiers kit, a lot of thought and careful planning was needed to get away with it, first I pinched a pair of sloppy overalls, the type that the rookies wear when not training.

this would help my disguise a bit, at least I could walk around the camp looking like a rookie soldier, unchallenged by the robo`s, as long as I kept within the barrack area.

overstep the area, and you get a beating, I had seen this many times before, I had taken to wearing an old beret these days, for a purpose of disguise, I had an idea, cut my hair stick it inside my beret, I didn't know how yet.

so they would think I still had long scruffy hair, bit like a wig, I could take it off, shave and look completely different, especially as no one here has ever seen me with short hair and shaven, and with all the things I had stolen.

This was my ace card, to escape undetected, and in a few days I could be far away as someone else, I crept into the barrack block one night, past the robo guards, and on searching around in a room in the dim light coming through the window I found some sticky tape and some scissors, I nearly shouted hooray, but just stopped in time.

"phew" I thought, "I nearly gave myself away that time" as I searched around I found some papers in a desk drawer, but could not read them in the dim light, I folded them up and put them in my bag, to read later, and with other bits and pieces, like a ball of string, a packet of biscuits, I crept outside, and made my way back to the pig compound.

Reaching the river that ran along the side of the compound I first put my overalls, boots and hat in a plastic bag, waded across the river, which was about four feet deep, and bloody cold.

Reaching the other bank I slid under the fence and crept into the shack, through the planks that I had made loose for this purpose, I slid in and got into bed to warm up, I was bloody frozen.

Reading the papers the next day, one was orders to train troops for search and destroy tactics, the other was a stores chit, for issuing clothing and weapons to soldiers, just the thing I needed, a stores ticket, brilliant, then I had a think, how to pose as a rookie soldier.

when, I had heard that there were more new recruits coming in a few months time, join them, yes, but first I had to get every thing ready, cut my hair stick it inside my hat, to look as natural as possible scruffy and untidy as usual.

After shaving off my beard, and making a false one, but sticking it on to look natural, this would be a problem, something I would have to work at.

I tried several ways to stick the false beard to my skin, but not much success, after an hour, it always fell off, the only positive way I found was to tie it on a string under my hat, this was successful, as long as I didn't go near to the guards.

My work mate didn't seem to notice any difference or comment on it, but he did cut his hair a little bit, the new recruits arrived a mixed bunch as usual, except one timid bloke with glasses.

He seemed to stand alone, not the usual boisterous type, I knew he would be picked on; this is the one that I would befriend, and get as much information from him as possible.

after a couple of days in camp and adjusting to army life, I slipped into the camp area, I had spotted the loner before through my field glasses, newly acquired of course, I knew which block he was billeted in, I made a bee line for him, accidentally bumping into him, "sorry mate, I was miles away, thinking of home, you okay" "oh, yes, sorry, sorry, it's my fault" he said.

Cowering slightly, expecting to be punched or kicked, "I'm Bill Daniels" pitying the poor sod, "he could be a really good ally" "over on C block ten" "I'm Dave Maynard A block six" standing straight and smiling, at having found someone who did not kick or punch on sight, we chatted as we walked around for about an hour, with a packet of fags, Dave didn't smoke, then the evening call sounded, this was a siren, anyone found outside after the next siren.

Which was about ten minutes time, if you got caught, you got a beating, soldiers were running everywhere to get back to their barrack blocks, Dave said "see you later" and hastened to his block.

I turned in the direction of C block after half a minute I then turned back, knowing Dave would be well on his way, and not likely to see me.

A head count was taken when you entered your barrack block; I dodged between two buildings, checked the air for robos, and crept out of the area, making my way back to my own piggy compound.

I met Dave a couple of times more, having got my I.D. tags and pass card with the blokes from C block, which was a bit awkward to do, but I did, and I was not missed at the pig compound.

This gave me an idea, put my pig mate in charge, when I told him of this, "me in charge" he beamed, "I'm the boss here" "yes" I replied, he was as happy as a pig in mud, he really did like the smelly things, as for me, only to eat.

I had found out from Dave that his block would soon be getting new uniforms and weapons then B block and C block, at this news I would have to keep my eyes and ears open a whole lot more in order to get my own weapons, and my means of escape getting nearer.

I kept a close check over the next few weeks, wandering around in the daytime now, I slept in a disused office, and I saw Dave early one afternoon, as I had taken to being around the barracks area just like any other rookie.

he was sitting on a bench, deep in thought, "what's up mate" I asked, but getting no reaction I said it again, and put my hand on his shoulder, I think he jumped six feet in the air.

"hey, steady on" he just looked at me, "sorry mate I was deep in thought, problems you know, problems" was his reply, "yeah" I muttered, and then I noticed his face, it was all black and blue, "been in a punch up" I chided, "who won," and I laughed mockingly, "they did all six of them" was his reply, and looking very sad and dejected.

"sorry mate" I apologized to him, "need a hand to get even with them" I ventured, "ha, get even, I'd like to escape from this place now" he retorted sharply, "shit" he swore, "you didn't hear that did you" he muttered in a whisper, "don't worry mate" I assured him, "I've been thinking the same myself, got any Ideas" I spoke in a low voice.

If you were over heard planning to escape, you could get beaten at the very least, whipped or even be sent to a penal colony, we wandered around talking in low voices, discussing ideas any that might work, we rejected walking out the main gate, no one is allowed out during training time.

going over the top of the fence, twelve feet high with barbed wire and electrified on top, no, didn't fancy that, "what about escaping through the training area," "hmm, I don't know we need to know more, one of my block works in the ad'min office, I'll see what I can find out" "keep out of trouble if you can, I'll see you here on Monday night ok" "okay, don't worry I'm on sick leave while my ribs heal, so I'm okay see you Monday" we parted, he to hospital block, me to my little den.

I had seen a map on a wall in one of the offices that I had visited during my searches, over the next few days I searched the offices, and found the one I was looking for, from what I could see in the dim light, was enough to know why anyone trying to escape through the training area was caught.

I swore, there were four camps, all joined by a high fence, and with a training area in the middle.

An area of about a hundred square miles, bastards, I thought, you really do mean to catch deserters, with no possible means of escape.

When I met Dave on Monday night, and told him of my find, "bloody bastards" he swore, "they really don't care about anyone do they, were more like the prisoners than soldiers".

"Yeah" I replied, deep in thought, "I could creep out into the training area at night and test out the possibilities of going through the fence" I muttered, "idiot you'll get caught" came the sharp reply, "no" I answered, "only the perimeters of areas are patrolled, you can walk out into the training area anytime, I've done it".

which was true, "it's only if you try to get out the wrong way that things happen" "aha" an idea occurred to me, "I wonder if our tags or passes are bugged, that way they would know where every body is at any one time, and why the robo's can catch you easily," "how can we debug ourselves" "don't know yet, have to think about it" "I could try" Dave was, full of enthusiasm to do his bit, "I've been assigned light duties in the main block, I'll keep my eyes open for any info I can pick up".

"Good idea" I ventured.

"but don't go and get caught or your for it, I've got training for the next week, I'll see what I can find out in the training area, I'll see you here in a week or so, on Tuesday if possible old mate".

we parted as curfew siren sounded, luckily for me, I always kept my tags and weapon in a bag at my den, so that's why the robo's never caught me, my luck has sure been in lately, but now to the task in hand, check out the area, and see what the other camps are like, six days to go till Tuesday, should be enough time I thought, after hiding my weapon and tags under C block barracks, I started off.

Once in the training area, I tried a few things with the boundary fence, throwing stones at it, as soon as anything hit the fence, a robo guard came zooming overhead, even when I cut one strand of the mesh, oops, that's not the way either, underneath maybe, I started scraping out the earth, then dived for cover in the long grass, just as a robo guard came flashing by.

"Not that way" I said to myself, luckily I had heard the hum of their engines, or I would have been dealt with immediately.

the only other option was through the dog compound, and I didn't fancy that nor did Dave when I told him my news when next we met, "bastards" he cursed quietly, "I go back to my unit in a few weeks time, and I'm not going, I'll shoot myself first" he said through clenched teeth.

"poor bastard" I thought, "he really means it, okay" I said thinking aloud, "lets see if there's a way through the dog compound, even if it means going tree to tree without disturbing the dogs, or if there is still another way".

"Not sure what yet, but there's got to be a way, maybe something we've missed, that the regime has too" "dunno" said Dave.

"If we were fully trained and had black uniform's we'd have no problem just walking out would we" "uniforms, maybe that's it, but how" I mumbled, with another idea forming in my brain, remembering a paper I had seen some weeks ago, in one of the offices on my searches around.

"Look Dave I'll be gone a few days, maybe a week or more, you keep our usual date at this spot, and I'll be back, maybe with some news.

See what rations you can store up somewhere while I'm gone, got an idea" I said, then I turned and left him standing there puzzled.

I knew Dave would be occupied finding rations and stashing them somewhere, without time to worry about me, so the following night I slipped into the training area.

My idea was to check out the other camps, traveling overnight, from camp to camp, just to see what's what; about twenty five miles in a straight line should do it, according to my map that I had sketched.

Maybe we could use the information to escape, I reached the first camp just before dawn, I was tired but glad I'd made it, I picked a good hiding place and went to sleep.

twenty five miles, a little bit out I think more like bloody thirty, I woke up ate my food out of the army issue that I had scrounged before I left, got the electronic binoculars focused and waited, as I scanned the camp I noticed that these soldiers wore green uniforms, which I had never seen before, I checked all day to find out why, but by nightfall still no wiser.

I trudged off to the next camp, same as last one got there just before dawn, but good cover was further away, in this camp they wore dark blue uniforms, and again by nightfall I was still no wiser, but I was knackered, I was not used to all this walking.

I climbed up into a tree to hide and catch up on my beauty sleep, I woke with a start, "what's up" I thought, a siren was sounding, soldiers were getting into floaters, which could skim along at tree top height, and quite fast, "had they by some chance detected my presence here, I didn't know".

Off they went in different directions so I was safe after all, two floaters passed nearby, I knew that if I moved I would have been spotted, and kept very still until they had passed, I decided to stay put until nightfall, then go to the last camp, but taking more caution this time.

On reaching the other camp which took me longer this time, it was already dawn, I crept forward and when looking through my field glasses, got the shock of my life, "shit" I swore then clamped my hand over my mouth, and swore silently, bloody black coats every where.

These were fully trained soldiers, "nasty people to know, not even kind to each other at times, selfish, brutal bastards".

I slept a little then checked the rest of the day, didn't see a robo guard anywhere, as night fall I crept closer to a barrack block, peered in empty, but I could hear a noise, peering round a corner I saw a load of them, drinking and playing cards, good I thought, I cautiously entered a block, found some boots mine and Dave's size, which was size nine, I went out and hid them behind some scrub bush, went back checked another block, crept in through the door, one occupant asleep, checked him, knife behind my back just in case, no need, flat out drunk, pinched a couple of pairs of trousers, went out the latrine window and nearly fell over a soldier, fully dressed and sober, I also heard a dog growl "heel" was the sharp command, then silence.

"what you up to" a harsh voice questioned, and a torch shone in my face, "shit" I thought "I've had it "er just a joke" I said, "wait till he wakes up" pointing to the block, the guard peered in, "hmm, beat it, don't let me catch you again, joke or no joke, or your for it".

"No" I replied, and scampered round the side of the building, luckily for me, I had put the trousers on as easiest way to carry them, walked smartly past two more, round the side of another, then crept to the end.

peered out to see if there were any more patrols about, phew, I breathed a sigh of relief, got to check better in future, I crept over to my hiding place, picking up the boots on the way, now to plan my next moves, and sleep the day away, till evening came again.

I didn't go to sleep again till the early hours, after timing the patrols, every two hours, "a bit slack here" I thought, "good, better for me" I woke in the early afternoon, checked the camp through the glasses, hardly a sole about, "can't all be drunk" I mused, but about five o'clock, four floaters came in, the troops disembarked, going to their different blocks, "ha, been on patrol, must be a transit camp, just what I need" I thought.

I got the hats, coats and gloves that night, from different barrack blocks, so as not to rouse any suspicion, then with the boots and trousers I stashed them in a tree, and marked the tree with stones at the base, I needed to get I. D bits and pieces, but that would have to wait until tomorrow night, I was tired and needed to rest, it's fatal to wander around here without being very careful, I got the I.D bits and pieces and hid them under a barrack block, then crept away into the training area, making my way back to my own little den, it took three days, I reached it at dawn, and slept most of the day in a hiding place I had used before, when I awoke I breakfasted on rations, "real food would be nice for a change" I muttered, it was getting dark by now and I couldn't wait to tell Dave my good news.

I crept into the barrack area, wandered around, no Dave, "should I go or stay, I'll have a quick check first then go" mumbling to myself, on wandering up the main area smoking a cigarette, I saw Dave, he was just strolling along, deep in thought, going nowhere fast, as I neared him I called out, "wotcha mate" in my usual way, he stopped, looked and I think he would have fainted had I not caught his arm, "what's up" he recovered his balance, and started to ramble on, then checked himself, "um, um, I thought they'd caught you, we had a right go here a few days ago, sirens, floaters full of soldiers, robo's every where, they'd caught a deserter out in the training area, brought him in and made us watch as they threw him to the dogs.

I couldn't recognize who it was, he was beaten up really bad, not sure if he was alive" then they gave us a warning "that this is what happens to deserters, dead or alive" I remembered the incident while I was away, "must have been some other poor bastard" I said, "less fortunate than me" and I "thanked the stars for my guerrilla training before I was caught".

I related my news to Dave of my skirmish around the camps, and especially the last camp, "can we go now I've got a pack full of rations stashed away and ready" "no" I cautioned "best at the weekend, that'll give us two days to get there and infiltrate, then if were missed, where are they gonna find us, in their ranks, no, I think not" "yeah I know your right really" Dave drawled, "but I just wanted to go" but just a little sad, having to wait, "I can go back to my barrack block anytime" an idea came to mind, "good, tell the medics that your going back to barracks, and tell your barrack block c/o, that your being transferred to another block, could even be a week before the paper work gets round, and they find us missing, better still" I conjectured, "We'll meet at the side of B block just before curfew, it's nearest the training area.

About nine forty five okay" and we parted with a nod to each other in silent agreement, I made my way back to the pig compound, and went in cautiously, it was empty, nobody around, furniture still here, wonder where he's gone, "oh well" I spoke to myself, and went to bed, I was awakened in the morning by my pig mate, "thought you'd left" he said, I thought quickly, "yes I have I just came to say goodbye" "I've been up all night with a sick pig" he muttered, "your doing well but now your in charge you can ask for some help later, if you need it, I'll be leaving tonight for good, and it's all yours mate".

I rested all that day, I needed it after the last few day's of trecking from camp to camp, I was worn out, evening came and I gave my pig mate as I called him, every thing that I had amassed from around the camp, I didn't even know his name, nor he mine, as we were just called pig men by the guards.

I said "cheerio" and crept across the river then into the barrack area, I had an idea to sleep in one of the offices, as my den was now occupied, I checked a couple, too full of furniture, a busy one, I needed to find a less used one, on checking a few more, I found an ideal one, office furniture stacked every where, aha, a store room, just what I needed.

I knew that pig mate wouldn't ask for any help until at least Monday, he was too busy being king over his domain, to worry anyone just yet, when I heard the morning siren, I got up and dressed, ready to go to the mess hall, along with the rest, I was bloody hungry my stomach thought my throat was cut, I hadn't eaten a proper meal for six days, only rations.

then I heard a commotion outside, soldiers were tramping along to breakfast, I put on a brave face, opened the door slightly, peered out all clear, stepped out rounded a corner of the building, and joined the motley crew going to the mess hall, must be about a thousand conscripts in this unit, I could hide well, got my breakfast, sat down and ate, nobody spoke, you daren't, all was orderly done, after I went out,

I was just walking away when I heard my name called, turning.

I saw Dave coming out of the mess hall, "glad I caught you mate, day off for me, what about you" "same" I replied, lighting a cigarette, we wandered around all day, discussing plans for the evening, we parted just before curfew, Dave got booked in, got out the latrine window and joined me as arranged, he was breathless and excited, but scared as well.

"calm down" I told him, "or we'll get caught, and to get caught after all this time and planning, no way never" "okay" he replied, "sorry, but I'm so glad to be getting away" "ok but your life depends on it, and you know what happens to the deserters that get caught" "yeah" he mumbled.

"let's get going the sooner were away the better I'll feel, right watch for the robo's, but first bury your badge and tag, then we'll slip away in your best army crawl" a robo zoomed past, then we slipped out.

we reached the wood in about half an hour, here we rested and straightened our backs, "be nice to walk upright" Dave muttered, nodding I agreed, I stood well, on checking my rough map and compass, I turned in the right direction, and started off, with Dave following behind, we kept up a good pace for three hours, then rested, "still got a fair way to go"

I said as Dave sat down beside me puffing, "not used to this" he grumbled, "but better than the camp".

We walked for a few more hours, then decided to rest, as it was getting light, we camouflaged ourselves in a tree, and slept, when we woke, and while eating breakfast, I told Dave what I really was, "a rebel" he just smiled, and said "that he had wondered, as I was not on any register that he had seen while on light duties, but I'm glad" he added, "sorry mate" I apologized, "but it was necessary" we made the camp by the third morning, climbed a tree camouflaged ourselves in and slept, I was awakened by Dave holding a hand over my mouth, "ssh" he whispered, "someone's' coming" cautiously and as quiet as possible we eased ourselves up into a sitting position.

I was a bit stiff, but daren`t move to ease the muscles, we could see someone scraping the earth with a trench shovel, peering through the foliage we saw a soldier from camp three, in dark blue uniform, digging a hole near some bushes, having done this he laid a package in it and covered it with soil, putting stones in a cross over the place, then he turned and went back to his vehicle and drove off, after a few minutes we stood up and stretched our legs and arms, working our bodies in a circular movement to get the stiffness out, "a bit of smuggling going on down there, don't you think" I said quietly.

Dave nodded in agreement, yawning his head off, as we all knew, drugs of all sorts were rife among the soldiers, and this was probably a drop off point.

We had to be careful not to be seen, "if nobody comes to collect it before we go, we'll pinch it, could be useful and to our advantage" I mentioned to Dave, yeah good idea never used it myself though" "nor I, can't stand the stuff, yuck".

we waited till dusk, nobody came for the package, I told Dave to stay in the tree and keep watch, with the night vision on the binoculars, while I went and got the uniforms and boots, as I passed the marked spot I moved the cross of stones, then crept back to the tree where Dave was, handed Dave all the gear, "freeze" Dave whispered urgently, "someone's coming" I stepped quickly round behind the tree, just as someone came up the slope, "phew, that was close" I thought, "good job Dave's got a vantage point" a soldier came into view, looked around for the cross of stones, couldn't find any, swore, then turned and walked back to the camp, "fooled his little game that time" I chuckled to myself, "I wouldn't want to be his supplier when he gets back, beatings all around I shouldn't wonder".

Dave joined me on the ground, "better get changed It'll be safer" he said, we got changed after swapping bits and pieces to fit better, we hid all the other gear in the tree, "that won't be found for a very long time" I thought, "now for the package and the camp" I dug up the package opened it, "sachets of drugs, just as we thought" stuffing them in my pockets, we then set off for the camp, Dave was nervous, "just follow my example" I muttered, "be as arrogant as possible just like them" as we neared the camp I spotted a dog patrol coming our way "shit" I thought, then remembering the drugs, "hope he's a user" but I had my knife handy, just in case, "what you doing here" was the harsh challenge, and a torch shone in our faces, a growl came from the dog, "heel" was the command, and then there was silence, as before.

slipping my hand out of my pocket, showing two packs of drugs, I walked towards him, "we were just out for a walk" I lied convincingly, he shone the torch over me, catching sight of the drugs.

"Oh yeah, and I suppose I haven't seen you either" he snarled, "cost you three packs each or I report you" "what" I grumbled, but it was just what I had wanted, I fished the rest out of my pocket, and handed them over.

"Now piss off, before I change my mind" he hissed, I walked on into the camp, mumbling to myself, and beckoned Dave to follow, "thank the lucky stars" I said.

When we were past the first barrack block, "first hurdle over" I muttered to Dave, "I thought we'd had it" he gasped.

"I wasn't sure either but I let his greed get the better of him, with a months supply in one go ha" I checked what's left, "I've got fourteen left, hope it's enough to get us out of here".

We dusted ourselves down, and tidied up a bit, then we decided to just wander around, to get the lay out of this camp, after about three hours, "just the same as the one we had left" Dave grumbled, we were nearing the mess hall, I was hungry.

"come on" I gestured, "lets eat" and entered the building, we got our food, picked up a paper, and sat down to eat, having finished our meal, I was reading the paper, and scanning the room with my eyes, only a few here, good. I thought.

we were contemplating what to do next, when an officer walked in, the other soldiers stood to attention, I nudged Dave and we did the same, he spoke to four of them at a table, then came over to us, "when are you two back on duty" he demanded, "we have two days leave sir" I replied, "good, at o'six hundred hours, you two can join my patrol, I'm some men short, and you can fill the gap" "yes Sir" we said, and saluted, like good little soldiers do, as he turned he said, "you will assemble in the main square, o'six hundred sharp, with the rest of them" then he left.

In the morning we assembled in the main square, having spent the night sleeping in an empty room that we found, and we were stiff.

"Right" the NCO commanded, "you lot have forty five minutes to get your breakfast, collect your weapons, and report back here, now move it".

And we did, everyone ran for the mess hall, we breakfasted quickly, and then followed the others to the armoury, we were given weapons, hats and body Armour, "must be a punch up somewhere" I whispered to Dave, on the way back to the square, "but at least were getting out" "yeah," "but we've still got to get away somehow" "I know, but lets take one step at a time, play it by ear, see an opportunity, and take it.

"now shut up before were overheard" I hissed at him, on reaching the square, we were told to kit up, which we did, looking a bit like ancient warriors, with leg, arm and body Armour on, although made of a type of plastic, so that it was light, it would deflect a laser blast, at least once, and you were alive, if you got shot, battered and bruised, but alive and o.k.

we were then ordered into floaters, fifty to each, instead of a hundred, the rest of the room was taken up by equipment, we sat down and strapped ourselves in, when we took off, all three floaters heading towards the target, we were told over our helmet coms, that our job was to round up a pocket of resistance fighters, hidden in a mountain range.

After an hours flying time, about three hundred miles, they dropped us at the base of a mountain, and we were ordered to march and to make a camp.

Some way up the side of a ravine, "I know these mountains" I thought, "this is where I was trained, maybe we can slip away here".

I know a few hiding places, we reached the camp site, by late afternoon, de`kitted, prepared the site, and sat down to relax, I was thinking of ways to get out of the camp, when the officer near to me and Dave asked, "two volunteers needed" "not us," I mentioned out loud, just enough for him to hear, turning, he ordered "us to go and collect the meal trolleys now" "yes, Sir" I replied, saluted, and pulled Dave to his feet to join me.

as we walked across the makeshift camp, to where the skimmer would land, with the meal trolleys, Dave said, "what you do that for" "I've got an idea" we saw the skimmer coming in to land, turning our backs to it, we waited, after it had landed, we took the food trolleys, and equipment out, and put the covers on.

After the skimmer had left and flew away, when the dust settled, we brushed ourselves down, uncovered the trolleys, and pulled them to a flat spot, where we began to prepare the evening meals, for us all.

we switched on the food trolleys first, these would take about half an hour to heat the food, next we set up the tea container, and switched it on, this would take fifteen minutes to boil, set the table and chairs for the two officers, the rest had to sit on the ground, when the tea container was boiling, I put in the tea powder, which I had mixed with the fourteen sachets of drugs, that I had left, "this should knock them out, for a long time" "good hope they don't wake up at all" we had our tea from a small container that Dave had put by, the buzzers sounded on the meal trolley's showing that they were ready to be opened, an officer came over to us, "well, open them up, I'm hungry" he snarled, "now serve us first" this we did, then the rest came and got theirs, while we had to wait, till everyone else had finished, even the lookouts ate before us.

by the time we had eaten, cleared away everything, and packed it all back into the trolley's, it was getting dark, and now most of the soldiers were drowsy, "in about half an hour they'll all be in cloud cuckoo land" I muttered to Dave.

"Then we can go" an officer stirred, and called up a skimmer to take the clutter away, as he called it, then collapsed in a heap on the ground.

I put him in a slumped but sitting position, in his chair, the other was already gone, on checking the soldiers, they were out too, a floater came in and landed, me and Dave started to drag the meal trolleys over to it, "lucky lot" the pilot said, "all I've got is cold food and drink".

"hey" I posed an idea, "there's plenty of heating left in the trolley's don't worry about the officers, they're out of it, too much drink as usual" "good" he replied, "yeah, I'll have some nice hot food and drink" "what about your mate's in the other floaters," Dave chipped in, "bring them over as well" "well done Dave" I thought, "you've got the idea, knock them all out then escape in floaters".

when the other two floaters arrived, we put their meals in to heat up, they drank our lethal tea, which had enough dope in it, to knock out an elephant, and we only had one hundred and fifty, plus three pilots, they'll sleep for a week, if they survive, I knew that some wouldn't, we gave them their meals, and mugs of tea, like the rest, three mugs each, of our special brew.

We waited till they had finished and were out of it, like the rest, I left Dave to check the floaters, while I checked the guards, they were out , Dave and me we carried them down to where the rest were, stripped them, of their uniforms, Armour and also anything that might be useful, we put every thing in the floaters, then began stripping the rest, and doing the same.

as we were doing this Dave said in delight, "see how they like it, hope none survive getting back" he hated them as much as I did, now he knew the truth about the regime, "hold it" a voice commanded, "turn slowly, and no tricks, or your dead".

turning slowly, my arms full of uniform's I faced a rebel leader, scruffy as usual, just like I was when I was first captured, some two years ago, "can I put these down" I asked, indicating the uniform's with my head, "their getting heavy" "okay" as I dropped the clothes, I stepped forward, and raising my arm I held the officers pistol to his head, spinning him round, I shouted to the others "to drop their weapons, or he dies" this they did, then I recognized one of them, "Diddy old mate" I called, then explained what we were doing, and giving back the rebel leader his gun.

"Three floaters full of arms and equipment, any use" I said, smiling, "o, yes" the leader replied, "very useful indeed, and glad to have you back, and your mate," he indicated Dave, "count me in" taking my pistol, he went over to the officers table, ssaap, twice we heard, from the laser, "that's two for sure who wont be making it back" he said smiling.

"Got any food left" one of the rebels said, "no" I answered, "only rations in the floaters under the seats" most went to get the food, not the best food, but when your hungry rations taste fine, "don't drink the tea or you'll end up in cloud cuckoo land, like this lot, come on Dave" I motioned with my arm.

"let's clear up and make some fresh good tea" after the meal was over and good tea was downed by thirsty men, it was decided to fly to the rebel camp, and from there, we could strike at the regime from within, now we knew the layout of their camp's. "death to the regime" I toasted, raising my mug, "fight for freedom" the others cheered, then we departed, leaving the camp, and it's occupants to fate, we were a happy bunch of rebels, with the future, in our grasp.

REVENGE

―――――――――――――― ⊰⊱ ――――――――――――――

$\mathcal{W}$hile walking around my house one night, in the dark, which I often did, I was quite

Good at it really, especially in the half light, and knowing where the furniture was,

I could do it quite easily and quietly.

I walked into the children's room, as usual, and I stood there, and as always,

Thought to myself, "what a lucky man I am, to have two lovely daughters".

Although one was fifteen, and the other thirteen, I still tended to think of them as little ones, probably like most parents, and would do anything to protect them.

As I turned to leave, I heard a faint scraping sound near the window, "bloody Birds" I muttered and walked across the room, intending to scare them away.

I peered out the window, and saw a narrow ladder propped up against the wall, But nobody in sight, then a glimmer of light caught my eye, looking I could just Make out a car light, shining from the lane, which ran past the house, about two

Hundred yards away, the light went out, "ha" I thought, "burglar bill's returning to Rob me, or even worse, I'm not having that, I'm not even going to give him the chance your scum, your dog's meat, to lazy to work, so you thieve and steal what other people work hard for".

I quickly put on some black clothes, crept down stairs, and opened the back door as silently as possible, before burglar bill returned, "must oil those hinges" I thought, as a little squeak sounded on closing the door, I crept round the side of the house, and just in time I drew back, as I saw a man nearing the house.

Upon reaching the ladder, he put down the bag he was carrying, tied a piece of rope to the handle, then he started to climb the ladder, on reaching the top he then tried to open the window, "now's my chance" I thought "while he's occupied" I crept forward and grabbing the ladder, Twisted it on it's side, causing him to fall, he let out a yell, and with his arms flung wide, fell like a ton of brick's with a thud he hit the hard ground, and lay still.

'Hope your dead' I said "your scum" then I went back inside for a cupper, feeling quite Proud of myself, "revenge, I thought, that'll teach him".

After finishing my cupper, I looked out the kitchen window, "yep, still there, but what if he really is dead, there will be an enquiry, and maybe his mates will want revenge on me and my family, can't have that, what to do, have to get rid of him" I thought.

"And any evidence, got to be very careful in what I do" I went back outside, first putting on some gardening gloves, to stop the finger prints showing, I took down the ladder and looking at it, there were catches on the sides, operating these the

Ladder folded up quite small, I put it into the van, not a car as I first thought.

Next the bag of tools, then went back for burglar bill, struggling with the dead weight,

I put him in a wheel barrow, and got him into the back of his van.

Luckily the keys were in the ignition, probably for a quick get away, I drove it down the lane and parked it in a field entrance, walking back home, thinking all the time, I checked the time, three o'clock, by now I could see quite well, as day break was starting to dawn.

I brushed the grass where he had been, watered down below

The window, to get rid of any blood, then washed out the wheelbarrow and put it away, went for a cupper and a long think, what do I do now, there he is in the

Van too close, there's a old shepherd's hut across the fields, no still too close, in the Woods no, a bit suspect that, "ha" an idea, "got it, the old fishing huts by the sea".

"Yeah, that's it" I went out dressed in working overalls with several more bin liners in a carrier bag, having already covered the drivers seat and liners over my shoes.

The rest would be to use when ever, I looked around as I neared the van, "nobody about, good".

I got in and drove to the beach, a bit cautious at first, the twenty miles seemed a long way, when we got there, it was getting light, and the sun would be rising soon, I had to work fast, but no mistakes either, I looked at my watch "four thirty, the milkman would be around soon" putting bin liners over my arms and overalls, I walked and staggered across the beach with him, like a couple of drunks. I dumped him in a hut, had a quick breather, no light weight to carry was burglar bill.

I got some of his scotch from the van, that I had noticed earlier, poured some over him, and poured some in his mouth, he groaned, "so you're still alive are you" I mused, I was glad really, right then, I poured half a bottle down his throat, with a struggle, but I got it there, as I went outside I trod on his fingers, "good" I thought, as I heard a crunching sound "a few broker fingers would stop his game for a while"

Outside I took off the bin liners and put them in the carrier bag that I had with me, I walked off along the beach to catch a bus in the nearby town, I eventually arrived home at eight o'clock, and checked my handiwork of the night before, no sign of any disturbance, "good" I muttered to myself, "and today I would get security lights and locks fitted, just to be safe, and to ensure that the event does not happen again, and there should be enough money left over from the cash hoard that I found in

His van, to have a holiday, so thanks burglar bill".

The next day there was a bit on the local news about a man being found drunk, and unconscious in fishing hut.

But had no memory of how he got there, and that he was being charged with burglary, because of the items found in his van, all from a tip off phone call, "good" I thought, revenge, can sometimes be sweet".

TALES OF FAIRYLAND

"*C*ome children, sit with me and I will tell you about the night I went to fairyland,

First I had to meet a certain Dwarf whose name was Huie, at the edge of a wood at midnight".

On arriving, the first thing he said to me was, "if you want to meet the Fairies, you will have to become very small, like a Fairy" I closed my eyes and with a sprinkle of Fairy dust from Huie, I was as small as a Fairy, then Huie took me to meet the Gnomes, who would take me to Fairyland.

They took me through a jungle of grass, and across a stream, then past a tree, which looked like a mountain, I hadn't realized just how, big things were to a fairy, I was Feeling very excited, for soon I would be meeting the fairies in their village, as their Village came into view it was all lit up like a Christmas tree, fairy lanterns and fire flies everywhere, with the sound of happy voices, it was beautiful, there were flowers, some I had never seen before.

The fairies were glad to see me, and welcomed me into their midst.

We sat down on toad stools with mushroom tables, and we ate Our supper which was cowslip tea and acorn biscuits, "mmm, quite tasty" I thought,

After supper I met the king and Queen of the fairies, Oberon and Titiana, were their names, they told me "that tonight was a special night for fairies, as they were putting on a play for fairy children, to show what could happen to them if they were mean greedy, and selfish to each other, and that I would be allowed to watch, as I could also learn from this, being a human".

The Elves and fairies set out all the seats, we all took our seats waiting for the king and Queen to be seated, then we sat, and now the play could begin.

The stage was set with a castle, and lovely flowers around it, there was great excitement inside the castle, as the Queen had just given birth to twin girls, who were very beautiful indeed, they grew up to be beautiful Princesses, one was a very loving and caring Princess, the other was greedy and always wanted more than her share of every thing.

The good Princess was named Wendy, and the greedy Princess was called Edwina,

One day the Princesses went out for a walk in the forest, here they met a handsome young Prince, he stopped and they talked for a while, but said "that he must go, and would return tomorrow to meet them".

Next day they met again in the forest, he came to see them quite often, while the Prince and Princess Wendy were alone for a few minutes, the Prince asked Princess Wendy "to marry him" and she said "yes" but when they told Princess Edwina their good news, she was very angry and very cross, because she had wanted the Prince for herself, she cried and cried in temper.

Then began to make plans to stop the Prince from loving her sister, Edwina had decided to tell the Prince that Wendy had told her that "he did not really.

Love the Prince, and was only going to marry him so that one day she would be Queen".

Princess Edwina made it sound so real; that the Prince believed her, and saddened at this he went away, saying that "he would return one day eventually".

While the Prince was away, Princess Wendy fell ill, because she could not understand

Why the Prince had gone, without a word, she asked her sister "why" Edwina said that the Prince had told her "that he had made a mistake, and that he loved her, instead of Wendy" on hearing this Princess Wendy felt very sad indeed, which made her illness even worse, Princess Edwina had to walk alone now.

She did not mind at first, but then she became very lonely, for although she was very greedy, and always wanted every thing, she also loved her sister very much, and now she also grew very sad, and wished that she had not told lies about her sister to the Prince.

One day as Edwina was sitting with her sister and saw how ill she was, this made Edwina feel ill herself, but from guilt.

And she dare not tell anyone why, but when Edwina heard the doctors saying that "Wendy would soon die, if a cure could not be found" they were baffled, but Edwina knew and was struck with remorse, and went to see the Queen, after Edwina had told her mother what she had done, she asked her "to help put things right, so that Wendy might live"

The Queen told Edwina that "she would have to tell Wendy herself, and beg her forgiveness" the Queen sent a messenger to the Prince, "to come at once".

"And all would be explained on arrival to save Wendy" after Edwina told her sister the truth, Princess Wendy being the lovely fairy that she was, forgave her sister, Edwina vowed not to tell lies or be greedy ever again.

On hearing the truth the Prince hurried to see Princess Wendy, and saw her every day,

Until she was well enough for them to marry, and to this day Princess Edwina never told a lie, or was ever greedy again, and so the play ended.

As the king and Queen rose to go the Queen spoke to the fairy children, and said, "They must try not to be greedy or mean, and never tell lies, or like Princess Edwina,

They would fall ill themselves, but to be like Princess Wendy" then the Queen said "it was time for the children to go to bed" and turning to me the king said "that it was time for me to go also, but that I could return again soon, to see another play" "and when I do I will tell you all about it, so good night children, God bless, till next. Time". Dee.

THAT'S LIFE

⚬⚬⚬⚬

*M*e and my mate Jack had been sentenced to six months in the local jail, not for being caught smuggling, but because they couldn't prove it, and we had told "the old faggot of a judge so".

"Six months for contempt of court whose got a big mouth" we should have kept quiet, what a laugh, "in this year of so called freedom, roll on 1780maybe that'll be a better one, as this one is rubbish".

Locked away in our separate cells, we just whiled away our time, one day I noticed a square in the ceiling, waiting until nightfall, I clambered up to examine it by candle light in between the jailers rounds, as I pushed up on the panel, it lifted up, "ha" I thought "a means of escape".

Climbing up I found myself in the roof space, searching around I found an old saw blade, and a chisel, left by the builders, "thank you men" I muttered to myself, it took about two weeks of work, gently sawing through the laths that the tiles on the roof were laid on, then fixing the tiles to this, like a door, which I could lift out to come and go as I pleased.

Escape would have been stupid for such a short sentence, I would be a fugitive and shot on sight, but no, come and go, do my time and be free once again, with a nice little stash from nightly prowls, "after all, you can't be accused of a crime if you're already in jail can you".

Jack must have wondered what was up when I sawed through his ceiling, "lord luv a duck" "I thought the devil had come to get me" "no" I replied, "just me, and that's bad enough aint it, come and join me mate, but first clear up the dust I just made, then make your bed like your in it".

When he climbed up, I told him of everything, "yeah, okay mate, a nice stash to go home with, but I'd like to see the missus and kids though" "yeah I'm missing Annie as well, but it's too far to walk in one night".

"As we scouted around, the roof tops, in the semi dark, being careful not to slip, we were looking for a easy way in and out, Jack spotted a window just open a little bit, in a house across the way, "think we can use that" "dunno" I muttered, "what about the people inside, we'll keep a lookout for a few nights, just to be safe" "okay" came the reply, and so we did.

Not a flicker of light from dusk till dawn, for four cold nights we watched and waited, "okay we'll put the roof plank that we found across the gap, and chance it, I'll go first, you hold the plank, and keep watch" "okay mate" finally we got the plank across the gap, after nearly dropping it twice, Jack held the plank while I crawled across very carefully, to fall from this height onto a stone wall could be fatal.

opening the window I peered in and listened, not a sound, climbing in I called to Jack "to follow" while I held the plank, when Jack was in we pulled the plank in as well, this all done quietly, then closed the window and curtains, lit a candle, peering around the room we could see that it had not been used for some time, thick dust lay everywhere, even the bed was covered in dust, "lets check the rest of the house".

This done we found it deserted.

I found some letters addressed to a captain John Smith, which I read, his wife had died and he had been left the house and its contents, in another letter pushed under the door, all dusty and wrinkled.

Which was from the captains regiment, it stated that the captain had been killed in battle, good I thought, then I explained a plan to Jack, "yeah, good idea, both our families can live here, while we serve our time, with you playing the captain if any one should want to know" "me" "yeah" muttered Jack.

"I'm too fat to fit his clothes, you're just about right" "okay" I grumbled, "but we've got to get messages to our families first, that's the biggest problem" well Jack was slightly chubby, although a six footer, but me six feet tall, just as broad in the shoulders as Jack, but slimmer.

"Yeah" I said, "let me think about it" we searched the house all night, and found a small money chest with forty guineas in it.

"Hey Jack" I called he came quickly "look" I pointed "forty guineas were rich, hey" I had with a sudden brainwave, "I could hire a horse, and we could ride to our families, and be back by morning, and give them money to pay any debts and the coach fare here, what do you think mate" "lovely idea, bloody lovely idea".

So next night I slipped out disguised as Smith, hired a horse for a month, with a saddle and feed, all kept in the back area, we were set, Jack was togo first, as there was a lot to sort out with his family, Annie and me we were childless, we didn't mind, we had each other, and that's all that mattered.

we had to get Jack's family in first, there was quite a bit of furniture, and the house needed cleaning as well, I was on my last trip to see Annie as she would be arriving soon, on my way back, fate took a hand, I had escaped from the local jail yet again, and gone home, but I would be back inside by morning, so as not to be missed.

But it gets a bit lonely in a prison cell, and I missed my wife very much.

It was as I was returning to town I heard a gunshot, and going towards the noise quietly, I found a robbery in progress, creeping around behind the robbers I caught the one from behind who seemed to be giving the orders, putting a pistol to his head I ordered the other two "lay down your arms" which they did after my captive ordered.

Them to, then the lady and gentleman stepped out of the coach, and after helping me to tie them up, we proceeded to take them to the local jail.

The gentleman went to the jail gates, while I untied the robbers from the luggage rack at the back of the coach, after putting them in jail, no one there recognized me of course, dressed in uniform and powdered wig, much unlike the dirty scruffy man in jail that I really was, after leaving the jail I was invited to dine by the gentleman and his wife, which I accepted, after supper he called me aside, and said that "we must talk" we entered another room, and after being seated with brandies passed around, he said "that he needed an officer like me, to do some undercover work, you and two other men should do, if you are willing of course" I said "that I was" "good I will give you a letter for your commanding officer, to absolve you from duty, and to join my company" "bloody hell" I thought, "I could be facing the gallows for impersonating an army officer, and this old gent is the chancellor of the exchequer, and with Lord North as prime minister.

Probably hung drawn and quartered, play it cool, play it cool" I told myself, "I'm between regiment's Sir at the moment I have no commission" "better still" he replied, "then you shall be my general".

I coughed and spluttered spilling my drink a little, the old man just laughed, "I'll be an officer made by him, that'll be legal good" I was thinking.

After a few moments silence, while I gathered my wits, I said to the old gent "that the two men that I need are in jail for contempt of court" "hmm, very well, ask my secretary for release papers in the morning come and see me when you are ready with your men" "yes Sir" I saluted turned and left the room, full of thought, "How do I get myself out of prison, hmm" so I left a note for the secretary, next day, two excise soldiers went to the jail to collect the two men that they had been ordered to, and deposited them at the captain's house, when they left, we went in and sat down, after explaining it all to Jack, he said "bloody hell, us excise men, I'll never live it down" "never mind" I said, "the wives will be pleased an honest living at last, and we get paid for it, a general's wage and two men, cant be bad" "okay I suppose so".

I would be known as general smith when in uniform, but just Sid Aires at home, Jack was to be my lieutenant, we practiced a bit me to talk like an officer, and Jack to always salute me, what a laugh we had, but necessary, we could make a good living.

And pocket some more cash as well; we could make it all legal like.

"We'll why not" said Jack "what's life for" so after a week or so when Jack's family were settled in, and Annie arriving soon, I went to see the old gent, our first task was to patrol the Dover road.

As ordinary men in the day, and to capture the robbers and foot pads at night, we did this for three months, caught a few, pocketed their takings, some we shot first, others we took to jail, we didn't like them anyway, ther're nasty, a little bit of smuggling from France is okay, but highway men, they rob and kill as it suits them, we were making a good profit, and getting paid for it.

We bought a manor house near Barham, and now our families were settled in, knowing that they were secure, made our lives easier, we sold the nice old house of the captains for a tidy profit, after a further nine months of us patrolling the Dover road, the chancellor sent us a message to see him.

On entering his chambers he introduced us to an excise officer, who saluted our ranks, "as you have been successful in catching criminals on the Dover road, I would like you to train a special squad of excise men, in the art of disguise like you use, and the method of capture" the old gent knew of our method, as we had shown him earlier, Jack in his disguise had leant against a tree in the chancellors garden.

To show him how well we blend in, "yes Sir when do we start" I asked, "take a months rest, then come and see me again" "yes Sir" we replied, saluting them we left to return home, we made good use of our months leave, nabbed a few took their spoils, and sent them on their way, now we could afford to relax, there was enough money in the cash chest to last at least ten years, there would be more, but not for a while, not with training the excise men, we had to be as honest as the day is long, or at least appear to be, for our own sakes.

We went to the chancellor's house as arranged, and met up again with the same excise officer, as at an earlier time.

We proceeded by coach to the excise camp near Dover, this camp served all over the area of the Romney Marsh flats, but we were to train only a few well chosen men for the occasion, "tomorrow morning we will begin training your men captain" "at 0800 the men will be ready Sir and I too" Jack looked at me and smiled, I knew what he was thinking, a bloody officer, huh, we'll give him a hard time, you bet we will, and all `cos we had run foul of one before, he did well though, and seemed to be enjoying it.

when we thought they were ready for the real thing, Jack said "lets give them a try out" after swearing them to secrecy, even from their wives and families, for if anyone should talk, even while drunk, they would be shot without trial, this they swore to, so two nights later Dover road, here we come.

We traveled the London road as far as Canterbury, then turned back, going across the fields, keeping an eye out for likely places of ambush, a soldier spotted someone sitting by the roadside, brewing up tea, as we went over the next hill we halted, "did you all spot the fork in the road, and a tramp making tea" I asked.

"aye" the all chorused, "well gentlemen, that's a typical set up, the tramp counts the coaches, and notes if they are rich, so tonight there should be a robbery or two in the making, and well be ready".

"Right lads, lets get to Dover and get ready, there's a ball in the town hall tonight, and people will be going home about midnight, we could catch a few men of the road" "aye" they all said, " lets get we'll fed and rested, as it'll be a long night, taking out these thieves, vagabonds and highwaymen".

Off we went to the barracks, and waited for evening to arrive, it came, we mounted up rode to the spot where we had stopped earlier, "Captain, can you spy from the top of that hill, and report what's going on" "aye" he replied, and scurried off to crawl up the hillside, "right men" ordered Jack, "lets make ourselves ready" having donned their sack cloth clothes, covered with grass and leaves sewn on, the Captain reported "that there were four men waiting by some trees" Jack slid over the top of the hill, and the others followed, while both of us, the Captain and me, we waited and watched from the hill top.

They were good, I thought, they should be, after six months training, I knew roughly where they were, but even so, I had a job seeing them slithering down the slope and into position, they waited until the footpads were almost ready to stop a coach.

Then they pounced, quietly and quickly, capturing all four, as the coach passed, unaware of what was happening behind the trees the four would be robbers were tied up and hooded, black hoods were placed over their heads, a bit like the hangman's hood, without eye holes, with their hands tied behind their backs, and a hood over their heads, virtually blind, this is a very good deterrent, and keeps prisoners quiet, if not a pistol butt does, and it keeps our disguise hidden.

When the lads came back to where we were they were all very excited, after all, this was their very first capture as a special squad, and the first of many.

No doubt their feelings were running high, mind you ten against four, but no matter, they did it safely and professionally, and that was our aim in the training.

We caught one other that night, but after a robbery, was he surprised to see the ground jump up at him, after a brief rest, we changed back into our uniforms and marched them to

Dover jail, two months later I had an occasion to address the men, "well done lads, now you're on your own, we have to go up North, to train more men like you, but tonight we'll celebrate, at our cost of course".

we celebrated that night, and we left for home in the morning, before being Northward bound, "well Jack looks like were going to be honest men after all, what you say" "yeah" he muttered, "it'll please the wives, but it's going to be a bit boring, but that's life innit mate" "aye, that's life my friend, that's life".

THE MINE

I had inherited a house and some land from an old uncle that I hardly knew.

Having seen him only three or four times in my life, but had always been interested in the old mine and the story he used to tell me about it.

The tin mine entrance had been bricked up after a cave in, two lads had gone in but never returned, despite peoples efforts to rescue them, after a year had passed it was sealed up and considered dangerous.

But it still intrigued me and I had always wanted to find out.

At the start of my summer holiday I went to the cottage in Cornwall, spent a week cleaning the place up and making myself comfortable, I bought two big torches that shine like search lights for six hours each, they were quite heavy but needed, and a box of candles just in case, I checked at the local library to find out what tin ore looked like.

There are lots of tin mines in this area, non working of course, all closed about a hundred years ago, I was reading about this and talking to myself when a man interrupted my thoughts, "excuse me Sir, I couldn't help but overhear your conversation" I laughed quietly with him.

"I am a member of the local historic society and you have taken over old Jamie's cottage, a small village like this everyone knows everything that goes on".

He smiled and invited me for a coffee where we could talk without whispering, we sat at least an hour, then he followed me to the cottage in his land rover, I made coffee and we talked some more, I liked his broad accent, he told me the whole village had always wondered about the mine for years including him, his name was Shaun, we were about the same height and build, five feet eight, brown hair and blue eyed, just ordinary really.

It was decided to investigate the mine together for safety, plus he knew more about tin mines than me, we walked the half mile or so to find the mine entrance, after searching through the bushes and brambles that covered the rocks we found it at last, not knowing exactly where it was.

I had expected a great big entrance, but it was only about six feet high by four feet wide, "before we break it down Shaun,

I would like to make a door to stop animals going in and leaving a mess everywhere" "he agree, I've lots of wood at my place we could make one ready".

We went to his place, a farm really, collected lots of wood, hammer and nails, talked of how it would be then back to the cave, measured up and made it bigger than the entrance, and with a battery drill, drilled the holes for the hinges, and back my place for making the door, "a slide bolt lock would do" we thought, and that was it for today, it was tiring work, we had a couple of drinks each then Shaun went home to get ready for tomorrow.

After he arrived we went to the mine entrance, put dust masks on, Shaun hammered a hole through the old bricks with a battery kango, a hiss of air followed, "that's that bit done Ian" "good now we can get on" while he hammered out the bricks, I stacked them on one side out of the way, it was dusty work.

We sat for a cuppa while the dust cleared, the door fitted well after a slight adjustment, another cuppa the dust cleared and a dust down, we put fresh masks on until the air gets clean inside.

We took the torches and candles, entering the mine cautiously, going forward looking around, the passage was like the entrance, it was a little musty as expected, the passage led into a gallery, rubble was everywhere, a passage way to the left was still blocked with rocks, we checked around the gallery, tin ore shone all over the place.

"We could make our own tin Shaun" he laughed, "we'll take some and I'll show you another day" I was tired by now and elected to go home, at home with a drink I mentioned "a day off tomorrow, as I'm not used to this much manual labour" "ok, see you Thursday then".

Thursday we started to clear the rocks from the blocked passage, but a huge boulder blocked the way, we could never have moved it without a crane or something like it, "I've a tree root winch at the farm we could try that" "why not" we finished for the time being.

It was nice to be out in the fresh air again, although it was cold in the mine, it still made you sweat moving the rocks, we went back to my place for a drink and plan the next move, I spent the evening thinking about it with a few drinks.

Shaun arrived in the morning with the winch and a large log on his trailer, he explained it all to me, another car arrived with two men, "thought we'd need some help Ian, hope you don't mind" I looked and thought a minute, "no your right Shaun, we'll never move the boulder by ourselves".

I was introduced to John and Derek, also of the historic society, at the mine we unloaded the trailer, pushed the log in on rollers, it was hard going but we got there at last, putting the log across the passageway entrance, fixed up the winch and started to wind it in, slowly but slowly the boulder moved, we pulled it out to the passage entrance then took a rest, after a while we started to clear away the rocks, a couple of hours of this and I was knackered, so we called it a day.

In the morning when they arrived we started to clear away rocks again, we worked all day with a few breaks, I mentioned about "having two days off as the mine was going nowhere, and we only cleared a few feet despite all the effort" we agreed to work every other day for the moment.

In the morning I went to do some shopping locally, "you're the talk of the village Ian" Derek spoke as he served me in his shop, we talked of tomorrow, several locals were nearby, "some want to come and help Ian" "well why not Derek, we need all the help we can get at the moment" he told them, big smiles all round, how many would be there next day was anybody's guess.

I went to the mine in the morning with a gang of men, all eager to work about twelve in all, who cares I thought there's lots to do, half of us clearing rocks the other half moving the boulder right out of the way, after a look around we started to clear rocks, in the afternoon one shouted, "I'm through" this caused a stir of excitement amongst us, at last I thought, but we kept on clearing rocks till the passage was clear.

We were having a rest when women appeared with a "cooee" they had brought tea and sandwiches, I think most of the village was here by now, I didn't mind really, we had put candles in all the niches we could find in the walls it was quite light, the torches we used when needed, we drank and ate then Shaun and I being the owner of the mine, led the way along the passage, "should we not have shoring timbers Shaun in case of another cave in" "I'll take a look later, now this is what everyone wants to see" he smiled, I knew what he meant I wanted to see myself.

We made our way along the passage then stopped, it went down wards at a sharp angle, the wooden ladder looked rotten, a new modern one was needed, after all had a look we left and went to my cottage, tea and coffee were made, I let them all have a look around, most never having been inside.

I let the women folk keep a few knick knacks they really liked, the cottage was full of them, I hadn't got rid of any yet, I rested the next day, just lazed around outside with a drink soaking up the sun, Shaun came and joined me in the afternoon, he left after dinner which he cooked.

In the morning I think the village turned up except a few old ones I guessed, at the mine we had to separate the sections of Shaun's ladder to take it in, getting each section down the hole was a struggle all lowered down on a rope, someone had to go down on a rope to put it together, Shaun and Derek went down with a torch, assembled the ladder and pulled it up on its ropes.

Five of us went down the ladder the rest followed us as we made our way along another passage for about thirty feet opening into another gallery, we looked around and found the two lads skeletons.

After all had seen them, sitting together where they had died all that time ago, most crossed themselves, it was mentioned to give them a proper burial in the local church yard, all agreed to this and it was also agreed to be them by the clothes they wore although in tatters, one of the locals agreed to do some research to find out their names and ages.

But first the police had to come to confirm it was not a recent crime, to be legal by law, after a discussion and rest with a smoke we checked over the gallery thoroughly, the mine went no further, no more passages anywhere, this done we made our way to the outside, sat talking about it all, the locals were pleased to have taken part in finding the lads, it settled a long ago mystery that all had wondered about, tomorrow was a day off, then sorting out props to make it safe before anyone else entered the mine, eventually they left and went to their homes, I needed a drink and sat with Shaun and Derek, the whisky went down well, the only talk was of our find in the mine, skeletons we had expected to find just not sure where.

We assumed they had died of thirst and starvation or even suffocated, after they left I dined and went to bed, tired but happy.

I lazed the next day away.

Thursday a constable came with Shaun, we showed him the skeletons, he was satisfied signed a paper and gave it to me, I'm sure he was glad to be outside again, he went quickly I smiled to myself, then Shaun and I with a laser tape measured the height of the tunnels for the props, "there's trees on your land Ian, we could use them as props" "good idea, got an axe" "better I've a chain saw" he smiled, "we'll begin on Monday then" "ok, no problem" he went home and I relaxed with a drink lazing in the sun.

When Shaun came with his chain saw he cut down four trees he did the sawing and notching to fit them together.

After lunch we took them to the mine, fitted six in place, "that's enough for me today Shaun I'm knackered" "I'm feeling a little tired as well" another day off then back to it again, we put up more props along the passages, "that should do it Ian I think its safe now" "good thanks Shaun" we went for a drink at my place, and that was it for a couple of days.

When the locals came with the vicar, they went and said a prayer for the lads; their funeral would be next week, which the whole village and I would attend.

I let the locals come and go as they please to the mine, they seem to enjoy showing others around and talking of how they found the two lads.

I went home at the end of summer, but would be back next year, I've decided to buy a new car, and give the mine to the local village people.

STUFF THEM

⚜

$\mathcal{W}$hile experimenting with electronic circuits, for a big electronics company, making military equipment, I accidentally made a force field, although small, I could not pick up the circuit board that it was on, a hammer just bounced off, with no harm done, laser lights, just veered off, at odd angles, like a prism, and not going through, so I took the circuit board to a local gunsmith, he fired at it with different weapons, but the bullets just bounced off, and the circuit board, it didn't even move under the impact, like nothing had happened, "brilliant" I thought.

After finishing the laser for night sights, which was my job, I carried on experimenting, with my force field project, I took it home, piece by piece, as security was very strict, after many tests, and taking out pieces of circuitry that weren't needed, I finally ended up with a small unit, that was the force field, and after many more tests, and checking width and height of the field, adding sensors to widen the field, and the power consumption, I finally had what I wanted, a force field to cover a body, which I could run from a battery, but to test it out, that was my biggest problem. I sewed the censors onto some old clothes, not very good sewing though.

I borrowed a shotgun from a friend, to go bird scaring, on his farm, which I sometimes did, and setting up the clothes on a hedge, I fired at them, several times, they didn't even move, "hmm" I wondered, so taking a chance, I put the trousers on, closed my eyes.

I was scared at this point, then fired at my legs, I didn't even feel a thing, I looked down at my legs, unharmed, "bloody hell, I've cracked it, eureka" I said aloud.

I even tried falling over, nothing, jumping from a tree, still nothing, didn't even feel a jolt as I landed on the ground.

"I'll have to try higher jumps" I thought, if I've got the nerve.

After putting on the jacket, and shooting myself at close range, in the chest, the only thing that happened was . . . . I broke my thumb, with the recoil of the shotgun, as I fired it, fancy me not thinking of that, and working with a thumb all plastered up, was bloody awkward.

By now though, the firm that I was working for was closing its operations here, and moving abroad, cheaper labour no doubt.

We were all given our notice, terminating our employment, a few grand as severance pay, and that was it, no thank you, or mention that any of us had worked here faithful and loyal to the firm for many years, develop many weapon guided electronics, made the company millions, and what it is today, myself included, I had worked here since leaving college, my first and only job.

"They're not getting the bloody force field now" was my first thought, normally I would have presented it to the firm to test, "but no, no way, not never" I determined.

As many of us were enraged at the poor treatment received from the firm, five thousand pounds was the highest pay off, I was as bitter as hell, "right" I thought, "I'll make you pay, one way or other" I wasn't sure how yet, "sell my invention to the highest bidder, I don't know"? Maybe use it to spike their operations, I wanted revenge, for me and my work colleagues, while talking with other work mates, during lunch breaks, I discovered that the firm also had a side line.

I sort of knew anyway, they owned a large retail outlet in London, "right that's my target" that weekend I drove to London, to check out the store, rather grand and expensive looking place, "I'll put a dent in their piggy bank, just the thing".

I had a plan, but I would have to steal the equipment from work, "that's ironic" I thought, "use their own equipment to pay them back".

So I used the next three weeks to steal as much equipment that I needed.

I had quite a lot, probably more than enough, "but who cares, I didn't anyway" and the last two weeks of employment, I kept myself as clean as a whistle, and because the security on the site was strict, doubly strict, and some had been caught taking equipment, and lost their redundancy money, instead of going to court, not me, I was Mr. squeaky clean, money seemed to be their be all and end all.

But first I needed a plan of attack, it took me another three weeks of planning, to find a suitable solution, this done, now I had to make a suit, head gear, and shoes, all to be within a force field, first I made up a computer voice relay, so that there would be no trace of my voice at all, if I had to speak, there would only be computerized words, then I tested out the new suit that I had made, my sewings better now, I had sewn the force field sensors onto a set of combinations, like a body stocking affair, this tested out okay, and with clothes worn overtop, the top layer of clothes would be protected as well, next shoes, I went and bought some black suede trainers, I cut the treads, mainly to give me more grip, and to disguise the make, painted some strange symbols on them, in red, runic symbols like I had seen on ancient artifacts in a Museum, "that'll give them something to think about" I thought, now for the outer clothes, I didn't want to be cold or hot, so I chose some black cotton working trousers, and a black cotton jacket, which I dyed the same symbols around the cuffs, and a big symbol on my chest, I was trying I think, to make a sort of uniform, as a disguise. Although a bit fanciful, the head gear was the most awkward, a motorbike helmet would be too obvious, besides, I fancied something like a Greek helmet, from the Trojan wars, I bought a fiber glass kit for repairing cars, and made my own, the third attempt was more successful, the mould that I had made of my head size was in cardboard, it didn't work very well . . . . but I got there at last.

I stuck the sensors inside the helmet with glass fiber resin, and the cable connector out the back, under the neck guard with the microphone wires, the shoes tested out okay, and the helmet with it's runic sign on the front, it looked great, at last I was ready, after months of waiting over, now I could get down to business.

On one of my trips to the store in London, I had noticed maintenance men going in a side door, with just plain green overalls on, and this was my plan of entry into the back area, which would gain me access to the rest of the building.

I booked a weeks stay at a boarding house just around the corner from the store, on the Monday, I watched and waited near the side door, nobody came, but on Tuesday morning, a van drew up, and out got the maintenance crew, four of them, two went inside the store, while the other two unloaded a large fan, then the other two came out, they pushed this large fan, on a flat trolley into the store, I heard one shout "where's that bloody electrician got to they promised me" "ha" I thought, "just my chance" I picked up my toolbox from the van, went to the door, which was still open "somebody want an electrician" I asked, "yes mate" one answered, turning as they pushed the fan into a service lift, "come on up with us, canteen first stop" someone said, "too right" "working in this place, you need a break".

After a tea break in the canteen, which lasted at least a half hour, the men set about putting the fan into position, and taking the old one away?.

This was situated in a heat exchanger, which fed the heating ducks into the store, "have to work overtime tonight mate" one of them said, after I had wired up the fan, and it was now working, "why's that" "loads of faults on your side of things" he replied, "give you a list later" "right" "this'll suit me fine" I thought, "get all my clothes and equipment stashed away somewhere, well out of sight, ideal" I worked there for three days, correcting faults and changing worn out parts, but not a finger print in sight, as maintenance men wear latex gloves these days, better still for me, no incriminating evidence anywhere, and with my blonde dyed hair, perfect.

The following week I did the same, except I could come and go as I pleased, now that I was known to the security guards, and knew the number to dial in, for the side door to open, as I was working away, planning things as well, I was called to the phone, "bloody hell" I thought, "who wants me, nobody I know knows I'm here".

As I picked up the phone and answered in my best Londoners voice, a bloke on the line said, "you want a lecky mate" "na" I replied, "I've been here for days mate why" "bloody firm don't know if their on their arse on edd, I`se trying ta get some overtime auta it" "no problem, I'm working late mate, like you say, stuff them before they stuff you, book to ten o'clock mate, no sweat ok" "sure thing mate, owe ya one seya" and he was gone, the phone call finished, I went back to work, with a few more thoughts in my head, next day I stashed all my gear, well out of sight, in a roof space that only I would normally go, having looked over the place, and worked out a plan of action.

Next week I would hide myself in the roof space, get my gear on rob the safes in the cash office, stash the money, and be away till next week, play it cool, move all my equipment, and disappear, on the day in question, I hid myself in the roof space, waited until ten thirty, for the evening stackers and cleaners to go, got myself kitted out, the two night security guards would be no problem.

I was a bit scared, but okay, I climbed down the roof ladder and alighted onto the upper floor corridor, I walked along it with my night sights on, as I walked I sprayed black paint onto the camera lenses of the security cameras, then I flicked a switch on a remote control unit, that I had rigged up, this would switch off the alarms to the cash office.

I hadn't been wasting my time, while I was working here, pushing open the cash office door, I stepped inside, sprayed the camera lens with paint, and proceeded to open the first safe, the electronic door and alarm were both disabled, with my remote of course, I put all the notes in small bags that I had brought with me, these would be easier to take away, in my tool box.

I hid the bags in an air duct, and went back to the other safe and it's contents, this done, I abseiled down the outside of the building, changed my clothes, got into my van and drove home, almost too easy I thought, as I went indoors, showered and went to bed.

Next morning I heard on the news, about a big robbery at a London store, and the police were searching for clues, questioning all the staff, I just laughed, and laughed, some people would have thought me mad, I had to sit down, as I had an ache in my side, from laughing too much, "ha" I said out loud, "I'll do it again next month"

I went to the store again the next week, as I went in amid all the hubbub, the robbery was all the talk of the store, detectives were still there, checking for evidence.

But could find none, not even sniffer dogs were any use, I had sprayed mace every where, to kill any scent, I just walked past them, went to the plant room and lit a cigarette, then carried on with a job that I had started when I was last here, I worked as usual for the next two days, on the third day, I met the electrician that I had spoken to a week ago.

"We've got a special job to do mate" he informed me, as we got our cups of tea, "yeah what's that then" "we've gotta go over the whole security system, and stay till It's finished, lotsa overtime mate, you on" I had a quick think "I only work for your firm three days a week mate I'm just a fill in" "well yeah maybe I'll cover for ya, you do the same for me, right, told the boss It'll take at least a mumff, he's okayed it, and the store don't care, okay mate" "when do we start" "today, now" "lets have another cuppa first" I agreed.

We eventually got started, by looking at all the wiring diagrams, for all the security and alarm systems, this took us a couple of days, and I still hadn't retrieved any of my money yet, "sod it" I thought, "I'll have to work tomorrow" not what I had planned, next day I went in as usual, and we started to run new cables alongside the old ones, as we worked up near my hide out, I mentioned to Jack my new workmate, "why put it right up in the top of the roof, when we can run it along this wall to the other end instead, much easier" "yeah" he agreed, "good idea, lets do it".

So that was that we did, we cabled up on the lower part of the wall, within easy reach, instead of about twenty feet up among girders and bloody awkward to work on, "time for you to go mate" I mentioned, "it's four o'clock, I'll be working late tonight, 'cos I won't see you till next Monday" "okay mate I'm off" after he had gone, I climbed up to the top girders, lowered some bags down on a rope, filled up my empty toolbox, which I had been carrying around all day, and the rest in a cloth holdall, like carpenters use, lowered it over the back of the store, waited till eight o'clock loaded the van and drove home.

On reaching home I put the van into the garage, out of sight, went indoors and had a stiff drink, which I needed badly, this had proven harder than I thought, but I was determined to carry out my plan.

After another three weeks of wiring up the new security system, we were getting to the cash office part of the system, It's now or never I thought, and we'll be finished soon, so I told my mate Jack "that the contract was finishing in a few weeks, and I was glad to go to pastures new, can't see how you stand it old fruit" "well its not for the job, that's a cert, just the money" on the way home, and back the following day, I planned the next robbery, much like the last one, if all goes well, I'd planned to work another week or so, then disappear, so the day which was my turn to work late, I did the same as usual, but said to Jack "well finish the cash office tomorrow mate, then the fire alarms, and then I'll be off" "yeah" "I'll miss ya, been great working together".

"me too" I smiled, "but we'll meet up for a drink sometime okay" "yeah" and he left work, "see you tomorrow" and I went back up to the plant room, at about ten thirty, as before, I put on my gear and went down to the cash office, getting the money was no problem, but on leaving the second time, pulling a trolley, with greased wheels, so that no noise was heard, I came face to face with a security guard, I'm not sure who was most surprised, him or me, he got over the shock first, and took a swing at me with his torch, which just bounced off, of course, then I hit him, as hard as I could, he went down like a sack of spuds, I thought that I had killed him, so I checked.

"No still breathing good" I dragged him into the cash office, propped him up against a wall, took his two way radio, just in case his mate called for a check.

I lowered the money down the outside of the store, this done, I abseiled down myself, put everything into the van, changed, and drove home, I put the van away, and had two stiff drinks, the adrenalin rush that I felt, was easing off now, but I was still a little shaky, "hope I can keep my cool tomorrow" I muttered to myself, as I went to bed, otherwise it's all been in vain.

Next morning I arrived at the store as usual, only to find police everywhere, as I expected, Jack arrived behind me,"what's up" I asked, "dunno mate" he replied, we went in saw the night security guard as usual, but were checked over before being allowed in, what's up why all the coppers" "We've been robbed again and my mates got a broken jaw, found him in the cash office this morning at about one o'clock, but we've got a description this time, what time you two go, didn't see you leave"?.

I looked at Jack, "we went about six o'clock, had an important date, leg over job, and I wasn't missing that for work" I lied, "go on then" he gestured us on, "police might want to question you later though" "yeah okay" we replied, as we walked into the plant room, "serves the stingy buggers right" I muttered to Jack, "wish I had some" "lets have a cuppa first" "best go and see if we can work I suppose, wait here, and I'll find out" three quarters of an hour later, Jack returned.

"Been questioned by the cops, they wanna see you now, just tell 'em , you work for us, and that we've worked together for about five years, and we left at six p.m., then we'll have a little talk later" I went to see the officer in charge of investigations, gave them Jack's version, and went back to the canteen, still puzzled by Jack's last remark, we went up into the roof space to carry on working, but Jack went out onto the roof, and I followed, the roof had a flat space, at the back, where all the vents are situated, turning to me he said, "you said that you finished at six, mate, but I saw you leaving at eleven thirty, I don't care if your mixed up in the robberies, but don't just say nuffink right" " yeah sorry mate" then I told him all that had gone on before.

When I had finished my tale, he whistled through his teeth, "bloody hell, mate, don't blame you, I've given in my notice twice before, but stayed, because of the money, I was thinking of doing it again, don't worry though my lips are sealed" "thanks mate" I muttered, feeling humbled by his words.

"If you wanted to start up on your own, I can cut you in for a half share, not as bribery but a thank you for keeping quiet, I'm only robbing them for revenge, and my former work mates, I'm not really a master mind thief, this is the first and last time, I didn't really set out to hurt anyone, just to put a dent in their pocket, the security guard I didn't like anyway, but he'll recover".

He thought for a few minutes, "I could be my own boss, then couldn't I, I like that, yeah why not, lets finish the job, I'll resign again, but for good this time, and we'll meet up later to sort it all out, right" "right lets get to it, and stuff them" "yeah lets" Jack agreed.

I sold my invention to the government, after a few tests, they were happy to develop it, I got a few million as well, and then Jack and me, we went into business together.